NIKI AGUIRRE ,

29 Ways to Drown

short stories

D1026500

lubin & kleyner
london

lubin & kleyner, london
an imprint of flipped eye publishing

First Published in the United Kingdom 2007.

This book is typeset in BaskervilleMT and
Palatino from Linotype GmbH

ISBN-13: 978-0954157029
ISBN-10: 0954157028

British Library Cataloguing in Publication Data
A catalogue record for this book is available from the British Library

The publication of this book was made possible
thanks to a grant from Arts Council England
Printed in the United Kingdom

Acknowledgements

Thanks to the following publications where stories from this collection have already appeared: *Mechanics' Institute Review, Tell Tales, X-24: unclassified.*

A great big thank you to flipped eye publishing, to my editor and friend Nii Parkes, whose support and mentorship has been invaluable and constant; without you there would be no book. Thank you to the Arts Council England for being so generous, and specifically to David Cross for his advice and guidance. A warm thanks to my copy editor Sue Tyley, whose quick, eagle eyes miss nothing, to Amane Kaneko for your fantastic cover art, to my writing group, Liars Cramp, who have provided much hand-holding, advice and laughter over the past few years; you guys are the best. Thanks to Birkbeck and all the wonderful and talented people there. And a final, huge, huge thanks to my friends, family and loved ones, who have always believed in me, even when I haven't.

Previous versions of these stories have appeared as follows:

Time Immemorial in Mechanics Institute Review (2005)
Flight of the Blackbird in Tell Tales: Volume 3 (2006)
The Little Man in x-24: unclassified (2007)

Contents

For everyone I've ever loved and for anyone who has ever loved me

FLIGHT OF THE BLACKBIRD

ONE SUMMER EVENING, in the middle of the night, my grandfather, Luis Alberto Ibarra, sent for his seven offspring and prepared to dispatch them to the hereafter with a Colt 45. This was their punishment, he said, as he lined up his children in order of height, for the misfortune of having a whore for a mother.

My uncles and aunts, shivering in their nightclothes, quietly stood where they were placed; all except my father, the youngest of the siblings, who began to cry.

Grandfather Luis was a neat and elegantly dressed man, a successful textile merchant with a penchant for pince-nez and pocket watches. His business took him out of town twenty-two days of the month, and though he spent the majority of his hours on the road, he enjoyed his work, for it afforded him ample time to contemplate his good fortune. He had a ravishing wife, a lovely house and seven healthy children – four of whom would one day take over his textile empire.

"When you are older," he promised his sons, "I will take you on the Condor Express."

"What is the Condor, Father?"

"Only the most marvellous invention! A sleek bullet of technological perfection – you should see her – glimmers like a bird on silver wings, but she flies like a demon."

"*Luis,*" warned Grandmother.

"When you are older," he continued, ignoring Ikela, "I will show you the demon in action."

To his daughters he promised nothing. But whenever he remembered, he brought them something from his travels: a little trinket or a sweet.

On this fateful day – the day of this story – Grandfather packed a valise, kissed his wife on the cheek, and several hours later, when it was dark, tiptoed back into the house to find Grandmother Ikela in the embrace of another man.

No one is quite sure what transpired between my grandparents. What is known is that Luis called for his progeny, lined them up in a row and threatened to kill them. Despite his accusations, my adulteress grandmother stood like a statue, while seven pairs of eyes burned into the back of her nightgown.

"What are you waiting for?" she said to her husband. "Go ahead and shoot me. But why are the children out of their beds? This is between us, old fool."

"They are here so they can see the tramp they have for a mother!" he roared, the gun shaking in his hand.

"What's the matter, Luis? Don't you know how to use your pistol? Tell me you didn't call us here so we can witness your incompetence? Now either kill me or release me so I can go back to bed."

"The only place you are going is to hell, Blackbird," spat my grandfather, his grip tightening around the Colt.

IKELA WAS SIXTEEN when Grandfather first laid eyes on her as she shopped in the market. Her shiny blue-black hair shimmered in the sun like the feathers of an exquisite bird. Luis was reminded of the Legend of the Blackbird.

The story goes that the devil once took on the shape of a blackbird. He flew into St Benedict's face, causing him to be tortured by an intense sexual desire for a beautiful girl he'd seen only once. In order to save himself, the saint tore off his clothes and jumped into a rose bush.

Luis didn't throw himself into a thicket of thorns, but he was so smitten when he saw Ikela that he ran out of his store and followed my grandmother, trying to work up the courage to say hello. He knew then that if he didn't conquer his fear, the image of her blue hair would haunt him until he went mad with desire like St Benedict.

Ikela came from a humble family of cattle ranchers. The only girl in a line of five boys, tall and fearless, she learned to ride as hard, climb as high and swim as far as her brothers. Her mother had died in childbirth and although Ignacio, Ikela's father, cherished all his children, sometimes he forgot she wasn't one of his sons. Ignacio's sisters rebuked him for this gross oversight, noting that the beautiful girl would never find a suitor if she was riding all day, ruining her hands and skin from being in the sun.

"Outdoor activities are for your boys. You must not let her grow wild, Ignacio," they advised. "In order to find a good husband, Ikela must do the cleaning and washing and learn to cook. She must feed the chickens and milk the cows. She must sweep the house every day and do the gardening. She must go to market every other day and learn to haggle and negotiate with the sellers. She must care for every living thing in this house, ensuring that all your needs are met, dear brother, for that is the job of a good woman."

Until now her father and brothers had done their share in the house without complaint. Upon being told that she would now be responsible for all of it, Ikela felt as if she had been put into a sack full of stones and thrown into the water. She wanted to ride horses and swim in the river and feel the wind against her face. But her father would not budge. As much as it hurt him to see his daughter moping around the house, looking longingly out of the window at her brothers, he knew in his heart that it was for her own good.

The only chore she enjoyed was the market, the only time she was allowed to take out the horses. Pinning up her long hair with a brown comb and putting on a shawl, Ikela looked forward to those long afternoons of freedom. She took her time choosing the weekly provisions and instead of haggling, she smiled her best smile and that was enough to win over the sellers.

That is where Luis first laid eyes on her and besotted with the pretty girl, he set out an elaborate plan for conquering her. He noted the times when she arrived at the market. He remembered her favourite stalls and what fruits she liked. He followed her, unnoticed, hiding behind tomatoes and cantaloups.

He cornered her near some mangoes one afternoon. Taking off his hat, he introduced himself, asked politely after her father and family, and invited her to have a cup of coffee with him at the nearby *pasteleria*.

As customary, Ikela refused and went straight home to tell her father.

"What a strange man, Papa. He has been leering at me from behind the vegetable stands for weeks. He thinks I'm stupid and can't see him."

"Luis Alberto Ibarra is a successful merchant, Ikela. Don't be disrespectful. We should consider his offer," said Ignacio.

"But he is so old!"

"He is a decent suitor and rich, too. He would be a good provider. He can give you many things. Don't you want a big house and servants?"

But my grandmother wanted more. In fact she wanted so many things that sometimes her chest felt as if it would explode from longing.

Ignacio arranged for the daughter of a farmhand to act as a chaperone on the days his daughter went to market. Adelida flirted with the man who sold lemons and was told by Ignacio to sit at the back of the *pasteleria*, while my grandparents sat drinking their hot chocolate. Luis talked about his business, explaining in great detail what his textiles companies produced and how much money they made, while Ikela sat primly with her hands in her lap, waiting for the hour to be up, so she could ride home on her horse.

A colleague told Luis that all women loved to be wooed, so each week, he brought Ikela chocolates, flowers and perfume, but still she showed no interest. He tried music, trinkets, and beautiful silk scarves, all to no avail.

Then, one day, Luis gave Ikela a pair of old castanets he found in the bottom of a trunk.

"Did you get those on your travels?" she asked, tracing the etchings gingerly with one finger.

"I acquired them in Sevilla," said Luis, who had never been to Spain. "Here," he said, thrusting them into her hand, "I brought them back especially for you. They were a gift to Doña Otilia from the finest matador the world has ever seen – the valiant Juan Miguel de la Sierra."

"Please, tell the story," said the girl, suddenly breathless.

"The legend goes that upon seeing the bella doña in the front row of the stadium, the matador felt his heart rise up and overtake his chest. Her skin was smooth like honey, her lips as dewy rose petals.

"Shielding his eyes against the harsh sun, Juan Miguel de la Sierra chanced another look towards the stands. At that precise moment she turned and he found himself staring into her perfect almond eyes. His heart threatened mutiny. In an instant he was down on his knees presenting her with the castanets he kept wrapped in a kerchief for luck. The castanets had belonged to his mother, the gypsy songstress Leonora Davilla.

"'Accept these as my humble gift,' he said.

"Otilia reached out with her white-gloved fingers, but then shook her head.

"'Will you at least come tomorrow and see me?' he asked, but his words were lost in the noise of the crowd. When he looked up she was gone.

"Otilia was at the *corrida* the following day, again in the front row, her ivory hair combs catching the light.

"Juan Miguel tried to concentrate, but he could only think about her eyes.

"The second time he saw her, he imagined she was covered from head to toe in black lace, with only her delicate throat exposed.

"The third day he felt he was drowning. He was the helpless sea and she was the voluptuous pull of the moon.

"On the fourth day, he no longer cared about bullfighting, only about seeing her face.

"On the fifth day, Otilia came accompanied by a handsome man and the matador felt the stirrings of something primal in his scrotum. He watched as the stranger leaned in so closely he was practically touching Otilia's lips through the mantilla.

"Juan Miguel's nemesis in the ring that day was none other than Negro Pablito, the fiercest bull in all of Spain. The crowd shouted its approval, but he only heard the blood in his own ears. Half-heartedly he waved the red cloth. Negro Pablito responded by snorting and kicking up his hooves.

"Juan Miguel glanced towards the stands to see if she was watching, but Otilia was smiling at her companion, her teeth like little pearl daggers.

"Temporarily blinded by a mixture of hot tears and afternoon sun, the matador stomped his black boots as hard as he could, defying the already-incensed bull, who had been waiting for this opportunity. As he turned towards the stands to look at his faithless lover once more, Negro Pablito made his move and the matador took a horn to his already-shattered heart.

"There was little anyone could do. As Juan Miguel lay dying in the dirt of the bullring, he called over an assistant and placed the castanets in his hand.

"'Take these and give them to that woman you see there,' he whispered. 'And tell her, tell her . . .'"

"What did he say, Luis Alberto?" said Ikela, tears streaming down her face.

Here my devious grandfather smiled, refusing to divulge the dying words. "Marry me first," he said. "Marry me and I will regale you with a lifetime of stories."

From that day on, everything changed between them. Instead of gifts, Luis gave Ikela stories. There was something about a well-delivered tale that made her face come alive. Luis forgot about giving her useless presents and instead focused upon the recitation of stories, poems, epics, bits of gossip and even snippets conversations he overheard on trains. When he talked of distant and exotic places, she took on a dreamy look.

Sometimes, like the virgin Theresa, she bordered on the ecstatic.

You see, my grandmother was possessed by a severe case of wanderlust. She was certain the grass was greener in other lands, and far more interesting than the same boring trees and rivers she saw every day. She was tired of the sight of the southern mountains, which were as familiar to her as her own two hands. In her dreams, Ikela visited places where there was ice and snow, and ladies with golden hair lived in castles that were so tall they went up until they reached the very heavens.

"If you marry me, I will show you these things," Luis promised. "Our lives will be one adventure after another. We will have porters and monogrammed luggage. We will ride camels and elephants."

"And where will we go?" said Ikela, taking his hand.

"To Egypt, to the pyramids. To uncover the secrets of the Sphinx."

"And after that?"

"The Taj Mahal where I will buy you rubies."

"And then?"

"To Africa, for lions and bears and zebras. And after that, my love, we will go home and make a baby. Don't you want to make a baby with me, Ikela?"

And the dreaming would stop for kisses.

My grandparents' wedding day was the happiest of Luis' life. He turned to look at his treasure, resplendent in a simple white gown with a wreath of delicate hyacinths on her dark hair. He was so overwhelmed by the power of his desire that his knees almost buckled underneath him. That woman will be the end of me, he thought.

He purchased a *quinta* for his bride – a large country house surrounded by acres of land and a little peaceful brook. He bought cattle, horses, pigs and chickens, and servants to take care of it all, just as Ikela's father had promised. Then he set about doing the two things he wanted most in his life: starting a family and expanding his business.

Within two years, they had three children: two boys and a girl. Ikela tried to tell her husband that three healthy and beautiful infants were enough for anyone. If they didn't stop, they would never be able to visit the lovely places he'd promised.

But Luis had his own dreams. He would sire an empire of strong sons to help him in his business. Luis continued to woo my grandmother with little gifts of stories. With each elaborate tale, a new child was conceived.

And the children kept coming. After their fifth, Ikela began to lock her bedroom door. But it only made Luis more desperate to have her. Relishing the new challenge, he purchased atlases and maps, travel books and globes, and scattered them around the corridors of their house.

After their seventh child, Ikela hired a builder to extend the nursery into a separate wing. It was here that she spent most of her time, hiding from her husband, her days a flurry of children, nannies and activities but, sadly for my grandmother, no adventures.

When Luis heard the whispers about his wife he couldn't believe it. Not his darling Ikela. But just to be sure, he started spending more time at home. He noticed things he hadn't before. Had she always worn a silver rosary? He didn't remember her being overly religious. She certainly seemed different than he remembered. Sometimes she sang songs to the younger children, her voice so full of longing and loneliness, it made him feel empty inside. Funny, he didn't know that his wife liked to sing. He wondered what else she wasn't telling him. But still he could not bring himself to believe that his beloved wife could betray him. Besides, she never wanted to be touched by him. Why would she want the hands of a strange man upon her? No, she was definitely not the type.

"You LYING VIPER, you harlot, you whore! How dare you!" said Luis, waving the Colt at her. "What kind of mother, what kind of *woman* are you?"

"The kind who needs a real man, not a desiccated dinosaur."

"Like the parasite I found you with? That low-life, scum-bucket, bible salesman? I should have listened to my mother. She always said you were *common*."

"Eduardo is *not* a bible salesman, Luis. He is an organist from the church and as I told you before, we were *praying!*"

"If you were both praying, my *darling* wife, why were you the only one on your knees?"

The terrible accusation hung in the silence for what seemed like an eternity. No one uttered a single word, neither a protest nor a plea. The only sound was the ticking of the clock on the mantelpiece.

Then my father, Diego, started to cry.

"Stop your hysterics this instant," shouted Luis, turning towards him, "or I'll shoot you first."

At that moment, the Colt leapt out of his hand as if of its own accord, and fired a bullet.

At precisely the same time the gun went off (Grandfather was later to say it was the hand of God), little Diego, struggling to breathe, fell to the floor, just missing the bullet's trajectory. It lodged itself instead in the clock, inches from where he had been standing, stopping time precisely at 12:42.

"*Dios mio!*" cried Luis, finding himself entangled in Ikela's hair. "Release me, woman! Can't you see you've made me shoot our son?"

Tugging and tearing away at the thick tresses until he was free, my grandfather pointed the Colt at his own temple and offered to kill himself if it made God change his mind and bring back Diego instead.

In an amazing feat of co-operation that was never again to be repeated, Oslo, Orlando and Otterdam, the three eldest boys, ran towards their patriarch and wrestled him to the ground. Oslo yanked his hair, while Orlando took magnificent swipes at the old man's knees. Trembling and foaming at the mouth, Luis muttered blasphemy after blasphemy, threatening to shoot his progeny in quick succession if they did not release him.

Quick as anything, Otterdam stole the gun away and flung it out the window. It fired a round into the portico, narrowly missing the cook who was eavesdropping, her ear pressed against the patio door.

Meanwhile, my father was prematurely pronounced dead by his sisters, who raised such a cacophony that it awoke Ikela from her stupor. She found the children weeping and holding hands in a circle, while her husband lay on the floor, her sons like Lilliputians sitting on his chest.

Ikela's curses were almost a relief after the silence, the words like incantations, each one growing louder and louder until the walls themselves shook from the power of her rage.

It was then that my father chose to make his re-entry into the world. Sitting up, the bewildered child rubbed his eyes.

The family stopped mourning and turned to stare at him, uncertain if he was a dream, a ghost or a demon.

"I'm *hungry*," Diego announced, fluttering his eyelashes. "Why are you all crying?"

The death and resurrection of her youngest proved too much for my grandmother's nerves. She fainted dead away. While her industrious daughters promptly revived her with strong smelling salts, some say my grandmother never fully recuperated.

FOR THE NEXT few weeks, while Ikela took to her bed, all the occupants tiptoed around the house like it was Sunday. After the doctor had made his visit and prescribed medication for Grandmother's migraines, Luis rounded up the children and the servants and gave a speech about compassion, forgiveness and, most importantly, about the need to maintain secrets. This was a family matter, he told them and they should *never* mention the incident with the pistol to anyone, not even amongst themselves. The servants were to cease whispering in the hallways and the children were to carry on making noise as before.

"The subject is permanently off-limits," said Luis as one of his daughters raised her arm to ask a question. "You are not even to *think* about it."

Taking their father's words to heart, his offspring learned to hold their tongues, hiding their secrets under their pillows like sweets.

Luis hired a team of builders to erect a brick wall around the perimeter of his property and had the doors and windows barred, so the purple mountains and green grass that Ikela had known all her life were now permanently obstructed by wrought-iron crosses.

"For protection," he said. "A man is supposed to defend those he loves from intruders, even from themselves if need be."

He put his remaining energy back into his work, doubling his business trips so that he was always away from home.

As for Ikela, people said that overnight the world lost a beauty and gained a monster. All that remained of her were her tresses, although no one was allowed to see her crowning glory. It lived permanently on top of her head like a snake, coiffed and coiled and ready to strike at a moment's notice. She even began to take on asp-like characteristics, her eyes cold and her cheekbones angular. A doting mother before, she now delighted in the retribution and humiliation of her loved ones, hoarding their shortcomings like poisonous ammunition to use later. She left the storytelling and singing to the nannies and locked herself away from the children with the same determination she once used to keep her husband away.

One night, a few years after the pistol incident, my grandmother Ikela Echevarria de Ibarra threw wide the only French doors in the house that weren't barred and stepped out on to the ledge.

Those who saw her said she stood like a magnificent statue, the winds lifting her hair and raising it behind her like gossamer wings.

Legend has it my grandmother stretched out her arms and took flight, a flock of blackbirds pulling her by the hair through the night sky, until she disappeared into the darkness.

Time Immemorial

My story began when I inherited a stack of my father's old Mysteries of the Unknown books. Well, he didn't *leave* them to me exactly; he left us. One cool Sunday in October, without saying a word, he packed a small valise, put on his hat and kissed my mother goodbye. After his departure, Mother and I didn't talk about it; we just went on, eating our dinners and pretending that at any time he would walk through the door holding a newspaper and whistling *Embraceable You*. But he never did.

I was seven years old and those books became my world. I spent long after-school hours sipping cocoa and sitting on the living-room floor flipping through the darkly illustrated pages and contemplating the possibility of ghosts, telekinesis and the Bermuda Triangle. I became obsessed the way collecting baseball cards fascinates some boys and football enthrals others. *Cosmos* was my favourite television show. Week after week, Carl Sagan would tell us in his deep, scientific voice to open up our minds and be unafraid to question the universe. "How can we put a man on the moon, but know so little about anything else?" pondered Dr Sagan. He was my real superhero.

My experiments with memory were inspired by an event that was to change the course of my young life. My teacher, Mrs Duncan, smitten with Neil Armstrong and an ardent supporter of the space race, decided to have class 4AD make a time capsule. She tried to convince us that the perfect items to preserve for posterity were a signed photograph of Neil beaming at us from the surface of the moon and a tape recording of the class singing *I'd Like to Teach the World to Sing*, both of which would be included with a little explanatory note addressed: "To the finder of this capsule".

As our class was a democratic one, we put it to a vote. I made two objections:

1.   As dear as the photo was, knowledge of history and culture was needed to be able to appreciate a smiling man in a bubble helmet, wearing large white boots and waving a flag.

2.   A cassette was just stupid.

"How can we be sure that, one hundred years from now, they will still have the right technology to read it?" I asked Mrs Duncan, but she and the entire class of 4AD ignored me.

I was outvoted 27–1; so much for democracy.

So I decided to make a *real* time capsule. But instead of useless photographs and toys, I, Albert Trebla, would preserve a keepsake from the attic of my memories.

"Don't you think it's weird that we call it a *time* capsule, but don't really have any time inside of it?" I asked my teacher. "I just need to find a device fast enough to capture memory. Do you know where I find a book like that, Mrs Duncan?"

She stared at me in open-mouthed wonder. "Albert . . . I don't think we should let our imaginations run away with us."

"A time trap would be an excellent idea, Mrs Duncan," I continued, flushed with inspiration. "That way your memories would remain forever sealed and intact with the freshness of a Tupperware container. Defying everything – old age, forgetfulness, you name it! You would know where you put your glasses or your false teeth. You would remember what you had two weeks ago for supper. Can you imagine the possibilities?"

Sadly, she couldn't. My teacher wasn't much of a visionary. Instead of congratulating me on the originality of my idea, she rubbed her temples with the palm of her hand and scheduled a meeting with my mother.

"I think our Albert is a little obsessed with science fiction, Mrs Trebla. Perhaps a few weeks without any television? And he should really be banned from those magazines he likes to read. They aren't very good for him. I recommend he read only good quality books." She pulled out a copy of *Charlotte's Web* from her desk drawer and handed it to my mother. "This is a very nice *children's* book and I'm sure Albert will enjoy it. It teaches young people the importance of friendship through respect and understanding." She directed a level gaze at my mother. "I hate to ask, Mrs Trebla, but is Albert getting the attention he needs at home?"

I stood watching them from the classroom doorway, clenching my fists and feeling my face grow red. I didn't want to read about the stupid relationship between a pig and a spider. My mother looked at the book, then at me and then at the floor. She leaned in and whispered something to Mrs Duncan that I couldn't hear and they both turned to stare at me. Later, at home, my mother put her arms around my neck, held me for a long time and then quietly packed my father's books and magazines into a locked cupboard.

By the age of eleven, I had two things going for me that most children didn't: I had a sad, honest face, and a mother who worked in a library. Forced by my father's absence to find work, Mother took a job at our local library stacking books. I spent my after-school hours there, doing homework and reading whatever I wanted. No one made a fuss, even when I borrowed books from the adult sections. The librarians would smile at my mother sweetly, making patronising remarks about how *clever* little Al was, whenever I was seen with anything that contained more than fifty pages. But I encouraged the façade of dumb innocence, because the incident with Mrs Duncan had taught me a valuable lesson: in order to eat bacon, you have to sacrifice a pig.

Still standing by my memory-capsule idea, I read everything I could get on the subject of time. I discovered my namesake Professor Einstein, and Dr Freud, J. L. Borges and H. G. Wells. I had to concede that on one point Mrs Duncan had been right: there was precious little written about my chosen field of interest. But I wouldn't let that deter me. If there was nothing, I would propose it. If it hadn't been created, I would invent it. I would become the pioneer of the time capsule, proving to everyone – my teachers, my mother, and the ladies at the library – that I wasn't some pathetic, silly little kid with air between his ears.

"All the best ideas are first received with incredulity and laughter," said DeContrare, a contemporary of Galileo.

From NASA, I learned that no matter how trivial or doomed to failure, all projects had important-sounding names, so I called mine "Saturn 1" – after the Roman god of time. I carefully wrote out my proposal in an old ledger notebook:

I. *To create Perfect Memory. Perfect memory is defined as memory that cannot be altered or damaged by perception, old age or emotion.*

II. *To trap Perfect Memory. To be sealed in a capsule for the duration of a lifetime (maybe longer, but that is an idea for another experiment).*

III. *To control Perfect Memory. To "hack" the mind and test the resilience of the memory process, so as to fortify against any threats and/or potential weaknesses.*

Before executing my project, I first needed to prove that forgetfulness was an integral part of memory. If you experienced a negative event, for example, you were more inclined to bury it and forget. This was called regression. If, on the other hand, you were always remembering a time in which you were happiest, it would be fair to say that the actual memory was not faithful, but an exaggeration based on your inability to let go of the moment. This was called several things, mainly perception, projection and nostalgia.

For my experiment, I chose an uneventful day and time, not a birthday or a Christmas (those are the days that everyone remembers). I wanted something characterless and ordinary, an easy and featureless slice of time that I could recall without too much trouble. I chose 7 p.m. on 7 July. As my experiment would include the removal of the nostalgic aspect, I decided to conduct it in what used to be my parents' bedroom.

One day I will be older, I thought, stretched out on the bed. I will look to the past to see myself as a child and recognise the single moment, which I had thoughtfully preserved in time. I was creating an infinite loop, a mental jump rope if you will, with my present self on one end and the adult I would someday become on the other. If I was successful, I would be able to time-travel back to see my young self, winking and giving me the thumbs up.

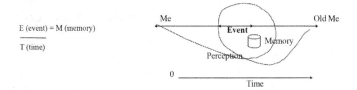

$$\frac{E \text{ (event)} = M \text{ (memory)}}{T \text{ (time)}}$$

I began by resting and putting myself in a trance. Sketching the walls of my parents' bedroom in my mind, I was careful to join everything together, not forgetting the corners, the ceiling or the windows. As with a doll's house, I slowly added in furniture and objects one by one, recalling every detail, every nuance. I painted with minute brushstrokes all my thoughts and observations: the colour as well as the starchy feel of the sheets, the comforting blandness of the beige walls, Mother's dresses hanging in the closet and the lingering smell of her Cachet perfume.

Once everything was perfect, I included myself. It was hard to know which observations to take, like packing for an important holiday. As a little kid I used to pretend to have bad dreams, just so I could lie sandwiched in the bed between my parents. Should I add that thought? Should I remember that emotion? I tried to make it basic, cutting off anything that linked to other things – anything that might get in the way of the purity of the memory. When I was satisfied with what I'd collected, I sealed the mental test tube.

I labelled this experiment "Project X". And I would repeat it again and again, 2,200 times over the next year. Every test was an exact replica of the others. If I forgot to include something or added an aspect that wasn't in the original, it was removed and, after a respite for clearing the memory ducts, it was conducted again. As purposely simple as my canvas was, the time and energy it took to put everything exactly into place was exhausting. But I persevered, because I knew, even then, that if I missed a single day, time would swoop in like a bird with a rapier beak and destroy the tender seeds of my memory.

Every six weeks, I compiled the results on coloured graph paper. After a year, the memory had become so instant, so well rehearsed, I had only to think of the event and it would immediately appear intact in my consciousness, a whole portion of a day redrawn in the whippet space of a few seconds. It was no longer necessary to concentrate upon the complex patterns of objects; I had just to recall the event and the images popped up, without needing me to recreate them. The memory had organised itself into an automatic sequence, intact and complete, like a computer program. Project X was a success.

Meanwhile, at home, things had taken a different turn. My mother, finally realising that my father wasn't going to return, accepted coffee from a stranger she met at a thrift store. A few months later they were married. Earl was a war veteran who spent an enormous amount of time drinking and gazing blankly at the world around him.

"Ally, I want you to be nice to Earl. He's been through a lot. Don't stare at his leg – he's very sensitive – and try not to make too much noise or monopolise the television."

He called her Betty (her name is Norma) and would leer and pat her behind every time she delivered him a fresh beer or a sandwich. "Betty" would act coy and sometimes he would kiss her straight on the lips when he knew I was looking. I couldn't stand how he smelled or the way he slobbered over my mother. Sometimes when he was eating, he would get little pieces of food stuck in his beard. I hoped my mother was only with him for the disability cheques.

IN LATE MAY, I came up with another experiment. "Project Zero" was the second phase of Saturn 1: an attempt to erase negative memories by voluntary regression. Being too young to have accumulated many of my own, I figured I needed someone more experienced, someone who had spent the last two years in the jungles of Southeast Asia.

"Earl, what was it like in 'Nam?"

"Ah, read your history books, kid. Leave me alone."

"Earl, I have this project I need help with. It's for school."

"Shut up, boy, I'm watching the game."

"Did you walk a lot? Did you carry a gun? Did you ever kill anyone?"

My stepfather just eyed me wordlessly over his Budweiser.

I bided my time, observing him out of the corner of my

eye as he stared vacantly at the television. He would make a perfect specimen.

"Aw, why you eyeballing me, boy? I'm watching my shows."

"Earl . . . what was it like to lose a leg in 'Nam?"

Earl P. Wetherbee slammed his can on the coffee table, walked over to where I was and getting right in my face with his veiny-red eyes and his smelly beer breath, growled, "Don't ask questions you don't know nothing about, kid. You might not like the answers."

I stared back calmly, knowing I had nothing to fear. I found it pathetic that he was trying to be so tough. Give me a break – this guy had trouble with basic functions! Half the time he couldn't gather up enough momentum to get himself off our couch.

"Earl," I said, "how am I going to learn anything if I don't ask any questions? There aren't too many people I can talk to around here. It's not like anyone would understand me anyway." I added sniffles. "I have to do this thing for school and if I don't, Mr Smith is going to give me a bad grade and Mother is . . ."

His expression changed instantly from one of rage to one of helplessness. He patted me awkwardly on the back, the way he had seen so many TV dads do to their sons. "All right, all right, kid. So, what do you want me to do about it?" He sat down heavily on the couch.

"Well, I have this science project I'm working on. I just want to ask you a few things and then write down what you say. Basically you would be my important *test* subject."

"What kind of test, kid? I'm not so good at tests."

Earl wasn't good at a lot of things.

"Let your eyes follow the crystal in my hand," I said after about the twelfth time I tried to hypnotise him.

"Hey, what are you gonna make me do?" he asked. "You ain't gonna make me act like a chicken or a dog or nothing stupid are you?" But as much as I tried to convince him, I couldn't get him to concentrate enough to take the leap. The myth of using gullible people to fall under your spell was just that: a myth.

We tried other things, but Earl refused to be suggestible. When I tried to block an event from his past, another would pop immediately into its place – a good example of the brain's defence mechanism in action. When after a few weeks we hadn't made much progress, I began to look at alternative methods. One proponent of radical regression therapy suggested we focus on memorylettes – the DNA of recall.

Dr Holcum wrote that sometimes the soft approach was not the best, especially when dealing with hard-luck cases like Earl. Strategic regression took years and required constant monitoring before progress was observed. Holcum suggested using the brutal hammer approach. Unfortunately, this meant destroying the process of recall: memorylettes, events, emotions – the whole thing. Sometimes, this also had after-effects.

"How much longer is this going to take? I don't think it's working so good," said Earl.

After two months of experimentation the sessions were taking their toll, leaving him listless and tired. He'd stopped pursuing my mother's backside. He was suffering from insomnia, nosebleeds and depression. His crying bouts would often last for days. When I found him hiding in the garden one morning, naked except for his army boots, I finally pulled the plug on Project Zero. I was sure that with a few more tests we would have made progress, but Earl was too unstable for any consistent results.

"Failed results, like successful ones, are always tremendously useful to observe," I wrote. *"More than anything, they serve as a blueprint for what you should not do next time."*

I WAS NOW thirteen years old. The school term had just ended and I was facing the prospect of an unbearable city summer. I decided it was the perfect time to begin the third phase of my project: proving once and for all that time could be successfully harnessed. I would demonstrate what Einstein surmised – that time was not linear. I called this final experiment "Time Immemorial".

As Dr Sparkling argued, "The mind is a super-fast and powerful processor, capable of taping and analysing every microsecond of our existence. It even records events that one is not aware of, categorising, filing and storing away the results in cryptic containers." (*Brainbox*, 1972)

**Cryptic
Memory Containers**

If I could somehow understand how these containers worked, I'd be able to access the process of oblivion and permanently store those memories I wanted to keep and delete those I didn't. In effect, I would prove that memory could be controlled.

I had conducted the transaction of hypnosis on myself enough times that I had no trouble entering the trance-like state needed for experimentation. The next step was a little more challenging; it required both brute determination and stealth. I had to barge through bolted doors behind which sat not my memories, but the boxes containing the material that memory is made from.

Working hard to open the doors of forgetfulness, it took me thirty-six tries before I was able to travel back in time, another six before I went through my own insignificant lifespan. On the forty-third try, I went back to the day of my birth. Two more sessions and I continued past the nine months of gestation, beyond my mother's memories of her childhood and the memories of her own great-grandmother. With each experiment, I drifted in and out of various histories, wandering past civilizations, past the lives of relatives from forgotten family trees, passing industrial innovations and hunter-gatherers pictured in my history books, regressing further and further until one day I reached a place where there were no longer any human beings.

You may express complete disbelief at this point in my narrative. But the truths of the events are as I am telling them. I had managed to go back in time so far that my world was now people-free. An empty slate, wiped of individual and collective memory, populated not with humans but with giant dumb beasts with killer teeth and vapid expressions. I am certain that if I had studied palaeontology they would have appeared less cartoonish and more detailed. Regardless, being face to face with giants was the most frightening experience I ever had. I woke up screaming and continued to do so until the teeth transformed into long hospital syringes.

It is obvious that whatever I said at that moment I regained consciousness must have sounded like hysterical gibberish. The leading expert on my case, Dr Franklin, was like Mrs Duncan all over again. He sternly suggested to my mother that I be kept away from my beloved notebooks. They were not good for me. He thought I was suffering from depression brought on by extreme attacks of nerves and anxiety. I was weak as well as anaemic, experiencing blinding migraines and nosebleeds. He suggested therapeutic rest. He knew a lovely place by the seaside where I could sit inactive in the sun and listen to the waves lap up the beach. They both leaned in to whisper, casting quick glances in my direction.

The attendants at Morning Tide didn't dress in uniform. Instead they walked around in T-shirts and shorts just like guidance counsellors. Everything had an air of contrived relaxation about it, as if we had chosen to spend our summers there rather than been sent by our doctors. But I was not fooled; beneath their friendly demeanour, the staff were sour and humourless, a bunch of Nurse Ratcheds.

The few times my mother came to visit, accompanied by an unwilling Earl ("I don't like hospitals, Betty"), she declined to discuss what had happened, pretending that instead of a fancy rest home, her son was at a summer camp, stencilling leather wallets and learning how to tie proper sea knots. She would never know I was having trouble sleeping, afraid that I had unlocked the doors to madness.

TWO MONTHS LATER, I was sent back home with a tan and an abnormally high prescription of Lorazepam. But despite the heavy medication, I continued to suffer from flashbacks that landed me back in the worlds I had visited previously. It all began to resemble a bad movie in which my subconscious had gained control, dislodging locks and throwing wide open the doors to my inner sanctum, letting in every ghost memory to haunt me, first in my sleeping hours and then when I was awake. Some days it was like experiencing déjà vu, the events looping round and round until I felt so dizzy I had to look in my notebooks to gain some orientation of time and space.

One Saturday afternoon, while I was reading in the living room, everything around me slowly began to disappear; first the television, then the bookshelves and sofa, until I was sitting in the midst not of leafy trees, or past civilizations, but in absolute emptiness. The absence of everything real and imagined is a terrible thing. I have never experienced such aloneness. Time as a concept did not exist here. It was as if everything I knew had been stripped to its most basic form and I was staring into the face of the unknown universe.

NOW THE EARTH WAS FORMLESS AND EMPTY, DARKNESS WAS OVER THE SURFACE OF THE DEEP – GENESIS 1:2.

I STAYED THERE for what seemed like for ever, trapped in the spider-web of my own darkness with only my imagination to keep me company. Rationale and sanity were pulled and distorted like salt-water toffee, stretching with pastel colours into infinity. I tried to scream but found I had no mouth. This was a fate far worse than death.

I noticed a breath that was not my own, a breath rasping out of synchronicity with mine, as if something were fighting or dying. I could feel the presence watching me from the other end of the room. I tried to stay calm, to still the beating of my heart. Then it started to move towards me. I could not see it, but could smell the stench of it – like the smell of sulphur and the odour of burning flesh or fish. I heard it drag itself along the ground, a sound like a giant fork scraping a metal plate. I had no legs and no arms or I would have run. But the sound continued, growing louder and higher. I heard it behind and below and to the right of me. I was paralysed, unable to do anything but listen and inhale the rancid odour of its proximity. And then I saw it.

A face so terrible, so awful. The face of all my nightmares put together was standing three inches from my mouth, dripping acid-like substance on to my skin. It loomed with red-rimmed eyes so hideous and all-knowing, that I tried to claw at it with my useless fingers, tearing away what appeared to be layer after layer of seared, deadened flesh.

I AM THE FIRST AND THE LAST. I AM THE LIVING ONE; I WAS DEAD, AND BEHOLD I AM ALIVE FOR EVER AND EVER. AND I HOLD THE KEYS OF DEATH AND HADES – REVELATION 1:17-18.

I was not religious, but I called upon God to kill me, to take me from the indescribable horror before me. And then the thing opened wide its jaws and I saw within a dark hole of nothingness that went down for ever like a well in time. At the bottom stood a boy staring out at me from the darkness. He had gaping holes for eyes.

THAT IS ALL I remember. A few days later I awoke strapped to a hospital bed.

I am not too clear about the details after that. I had to be subdued and heavily medicated by two large orderlies because I refused to sleep. One of them was named Scott. It was stitched on the pocket of his white uniform.

"Scott, why can't I stay up? I'm not tired. Please, I promise not to make any noise. No, don't turn off the light. Scott! I don't like it when it's dark."

Alone afterwards in my cot, I heard whispers coming from the corridor outside my room.

". . . no recollection . . . neurosynapses of an eighty-five-year-old . . . cerebral hippocampus . . ."

Sometimes medical words can sound like poetry. It must be the Latin root. I think it would be nice to be a doctor. I would make a *great* doctor. Maybe I'd get some books out from the library. . .

". . . verge of verebiticosiac collapse . . . abnormal cell conflux . . ."

I struggled to listen to their conversation, but my head felt heavy and the voices started to sound strange, like someone was pressing fast forward on a tape recorder. "Albert Trebla, AlbertTreblalbertreblalbertrebla," the voices screeched. "His name is a palindrome."

DR CORRIE HAS changed my medication again. He is trying to cure me of my "somnophobia", which is what he likes to call the night terrors. I have told him this term is highly inaccurate, as I am haunted in the daytime as well as the night.

The dreams come in the twilight state between sleep and consciousness, transporting me back to that Tuesday, still innocent and untouched in its silver capsule. I see my seven-year-old self, lying on my parents' bed, a hand held up in a brief immortal salute to the future.

But lately the eyes of the boy are not my own. They have become the eyes of another. The other day they were the red eyes of Earl.

Sometimes, I barely have enough time to wave before I am taken kicking and screaming into a world of my deepest nightmares. A world in which a little boy is playing with the hands of time.

Despite this, I don't have many complaints. I am well tended and the food, while by no means appetising, is plentiful. The doctors say I am making real progress. They say if I continue to co-operate, and with some hard work, I might be out of here soon. My only wish is that my mother would come and visit. I no longer remember how long it's been since I've seen her.

I don't want to be alone on another fourteenth birthday.

SCALING MACCHU PICCHU

IT WAS ALMOST midnight when Dooley arrived at the Lucky Buddha, wearing a long scarf and beige overcoat and looking as if she were on an undercover mission.

She seated herself across from me, ordered a pot of jasmine tea and put her hand on top of mine. "So," she whispered, her excitement visible even in the dimness of the restaurant's red-leatherette interior, "did you ask me here to talk about *him*? Did Matthew call?"

Dr Dorothy Monroe, a.k.a. Dooley, esteemed professor of film studies and the author of three well-respected books in her field, was my best friend and one of the foremost experts in cheesy dramas – including the particulars of my own life. Bad lighting, low production values, hammy acting and cringe-worthy storylines were de rigueur. The more appalling the storyline, the more Dooley loved it.

"Since when do you drink whisky, Elsa?" She indicated my half-empty glass. "You're practically a teetotaller."

"I drink from time to time," I said. "You've just never noticed."

"Well, I would join you, but I have to be up early tomorrow.

Look, on the phone you said you needed to discuss something important. I thought it was about him, so I came immediately. You interrupted me in the middle of a retrospective – *Columbo: The Man Under the Hat* – so this had better be good."

"This has nothing to do with Matthew," I said. "I haven't heard from him in months." I took a long swallow of my Chivas. It burned the back of my throat like fire. My impulse was to cough and splutter, but I didn't want to give Dooley the pleasure. "So, how are your students this term?" I said when I could speak again.

"There is one young man who has potential. One student out of one hundred and thirty, can you believe it?" She unwrapped her scarf. "He doesn't seem to be familiar with anything made before 1987, but his heart is in the right place. What he lacks in knowledge he more than makes up for in passion. The rest are pretentious, smug *children*, who think I should give them a good grade just for showing up to my class. Is it me, or do my students get worse every term?"

"You say that every year, Dooley. But it's the start of the semester. Give them time. You'll love them by Christmas."

"I doubt it," she said, taking a sip of her tea. "Now I know you didn't call me here to talk about work, so let's hear it." She stared at me with her infamous eyes.

Dooley had the all-seeing eyes of a mother. Although she herself was childless, she had mastered the look of stern parents and teachers known to children everywhere. The look that lets you know – faster than a Wild West sheriff at sundown, faster than a ninja warrior whizzing a star of death – that she is on to you. Penetratingly blue and direct, her gaze had that supreme confidence that came from being fluent in a language that needed no words: a language associated with traffic signals. Green: I have deemed you acceptable; amber: proceed with caution; red: well, let's just say you didn't want them to be red.

I played with my chopsticks and avoided Dooley's eyes.

I was about to reveal the purpose of our late-night tête-à-tête, when Mr Lee, the proprietor of the Lucky Buddha, came by to say hello, placing a plate of fried wontons on the table accompanied by a pot of his special plum sauce.

"To be shared between you," he said, arranging the wontons in the middle, as if we were greedy little girls.

Mr Lee seemed to have no concept of time. He never looked surprised to see us, no matter how infrequent or untimely our visits over the last few years. He didn't utter trite clichés or make useless small talk the way people do when they don't know what else to say. As far as Mr Lee was concerned, every one of our visits was part of an extended day that had lasted eight years.

The first time I met Dooley was at a Starbucks around the corner from my university. I was a second-year film student in the throes of my first big relationship. Roman was everything I always wanted in a boyfriend: good-looking, opinionated, indifferent and aloof. He was a graduate student who floored me with his knowledge of films and literature. As we didn't have much money, most of our dates were over coffee, where I spent hours staring into his eyes and pretending to listen to him talk about German cinema.

Predictably, he took me to Starbucks when he decided to dump me. Trying hard not to cry into my latte, I asked all the usual questions, blaming myself for my inability to be the perfect girlfriend.

"It isn't you, Elsa," he said, with a magnanimous wave of his hand.

"But you said you *loved* me. Why did you say you loved me if you weren't sure?"

"Look, you're young. You're just starting out. I'm at a *different* stage. For God's sake, you've never even heard of *Fassbinder*. I'm sorry, but this just isn't going to work out."

He drained his espresso and walked out of the coffee house without looking back.

I was so distraught, feeling as if the guts had been yanked out of me, that I hadn't noticed the blond woman at the nearby table.

"Fassbinder is overrated in my opinion," she said.

"Excuse me?"

"Other than *Despair*, his work is avant-garde, very *enfant terrible*. No wonder he appeals to your boyfriend."

"*Ex*-boyfriend," I sobbed.

"How long were you two going out?"

"Four months, two weeks and five days," I said miserably.

"Well, in my opinion, that much time deserves better than a public coffee-house break-up."

I blew my nose on a paper napkin and nodded.

"Mind if I come over and sit?" the blonde said, packing up her tea, books and papers and stuffing them into an oversized handbag. "Listen, I know it feels awful right now, but he's right about one thing. You are just a kid. You have your whole life ahead of you and four months is too long to spend hung up on someone who doesn't know how to treat you."

I nodded again and made room for her at my table.

"Shall we trade bad break-up stories? June 1979, my senior year, Delray Devon – seriously, that was his name – decides to dump me two hours before prom. Two hours! I'd spent every spare hour working at a roadhouse diner to save up for my dress. It was beautiful – pink ribbons against velvet black with a scoop neck and puffy sleeves. I still have that dress," she said fondly. "Anyway, the bastard dumps me for Monica Scalata, dark-haired, curvy girl. You know the type: cheerleader, debate team, honour society – a real bitch. Instead of the wonderful night I'd envisioned, dancing under the stars, I spent it in my room, my stomach burning from jealousy pangs. But . . . there is a point to my story."

I waited to hear what she had to say, grateful that for the moment I had something else to think about besides being dumped by Roman.

"After my self-indulgent fit, I washed my face, combed my hair, threw a sweater over my prom dress and went to the movies, *by myself*. I watched a fright-night double feature: *Dawn of the Dead* and *Alien*. Glorious. I forgot all about Delon."

"You mean *Delray*."

"Yes, of course. Most importantly, I learned that films can cure all maladies: despair, heartbreak, yearning. A few hours in the dark with someone else's tragedies and you feel restored, almost brand new."

She shook her blond ringlets. Her hair was short and curly. Two mismatched plastic barrettes clamped either side of her head: one in the shape of a seahorse, the other a cat of some sort. It was an odd choice of hairdo, even for this strange woman, and I wondered whether the hairclips were a statement of irony or if she actually thought they worked.

"I'm Dr Monroe by the way, 'Dooley' if you please. I just started teaching at Glendale: Contemporary Cinema."

"Really? That's great."

"What are you studying this term?"

"European film Studies. But, can I be honest? I find it dead boring."

"Not that I was eavesdropping, but I gathered as much from your conversation with Mr Dashing."

"What I really want to sink my teeth into is scriptwriting. I want to write visual stories. Not black-and-white, artsy-fartsy, three-hour-long productions about misunderstood circus folks or how a flying trapeze symbolises man's existential dilemma. I want colour, dialogue and action. I want to be grabbed and thrown around the cinema like a rag doll. Otherwise, what is the point of creating anything?"

Dooley sat back, her eyes shining.

"I tell you what . . ." She pulled out a crumpled newspaper from her purse. "I don't know if you like Keanu Reeves, but I've been dying to see *The Matrix*. What do you say?"

Having nothing better to do, I went. Afterwards we ate at the Lucky Buddha, the restaurant around the corner from the cinema. Over countless pots of jasmine tea, we dissected the plot, sparing nothing: not Keanu's acting, the Hollywood-ised concept of virtual worlds, nor the extraordinary stunts. I'd always wanted to have a friend to do that with, and here she was, sitting across from me, brighter and more vivid than anything on celluloid.

Over our first plate of wontons, I learned that Dooley was invincible. She could swear in six different languages, ran five miles each day, poured ice-cold vodka down her throat like a Polish sailor and unashamedly wore the emotional scars of the walking wounded. In her own words, she was a pansexual polymorph: a fluent lover and a frequent failure in equal measures.

During the salad days of our friendship, we usually caught a movie and then dinner at the Buddha. It was cheap and its womb-like interior was perfect for analysing all the minute details of our lives and the in-between moments. But the real reason we continued to come to this little Chinese restaurant at the edge of town with its Formica tables and its tattered red lanterns – even after I'd graduated and Dooley had moved on to other colleges – was because this place was our way of coping with the uncertain world of revolving doors and surprises. The Buddha was the panacea for the inevitabilities that consumed us.

Over the years, the restaurant had been witness to career changes, existential dilemmas, scripting nightmares, Dooley's father's fourth marriage, her mother's nervous breakdown and my stepsister Ralphie's suicide attempt. It had been privy to abortions, inconsequential relationships, broken hearts; the surreal and hostile environment of academia; and Dooley's affair with one married Professor M. T. Mencken. The ubiquitous walls of the Buddha had heard it all, had entertained a long string of friends and lovers who made cameo appearances and played guest-starring roles in our lives.

Prime example: *The Greatest Romance That Never Was*, a relationship that was conducted almost entirely in the Buddha. I say "in" because although Matthew, the object of my obsession, had never stepped inside the restaurant, his every word, action and gesture – perceived and real – lived gloriously on in the Technicolor reds of the Buddha.

A thirty-seven-year-old stockbroker, Matt was an older version of my first boyfriend Roman, except he wasn't literary or into German cinema. His favourite movie was *Mad Max*, and apart from the single book in his bathroom – *Zen and the Art of Motorcycle Maintenance*, which he bought because he liked the title – he wasn't a philosophical sort of man.

"So, what's he like?" asked Dooley, after I called an emergency late-night meeting at the Buddha.

"Matt is . . . well . . . *indescribable*."

"What? That's ridiculous. You are a writer, Elsa. Surely you can come up with something better."

"Well, let's say his unique charm is that I can't easily categorise him. He isn't like anyone else I've ever dated."

She raised a quizzical eyebrow.

"Take for example his prized photograph, the one in the silver frame in his living room. It's of him with the Pope during the great popemobile tour of '93. But Matthew isn't religious, irreverent or the least bit ironic, so what's he trying to say? On our first date I sat on his couch, staring at the wall, trying to figure it out. I couldn't even concentrate on what he was saying.

I had so many questions. Was I dating a misunderstood genius? An artist? An idiot? All of the above?"

"Sounds like a winner. Remind me again why you are still going out with him?"

"Dooley, he is handsome, moody, brooding and completely unwilling to give an inch. He's a walking question mark. I'm completely infatuated."

"That's right. The whole hitting-your-head-against-the-wall sensation you humans call love. So, is the plan to get Mr Wonderful to fall for you? I can help, you know. I've watched countless films and can tell you what you need to do."

"Does it involve a makeover?"

"Of course. We will also need an eighties' soundtrack and an elaborate montage. By the time the last song plays, I'll guarantee you'll have your man."

"But how about the big break-up? How will I know he's the right one for me?" I fluttered my eyelashes.

"Don't worry. He'll realise how blind he was in the third act, when he sees that you were right in front of him all along."

"Then what?"

"Then you kiss."

"And we live happily ever after?"

"No, then the credits roll, silly."

"Can I be honest, Dooley? There is something different about Matthew. Underneath all the bravado and the aloof exterior, there is a spark, an atom. It sounds ridiculous, right? But I think I know what it is."

"So are you going to tell me, or do I have to guess?" she asked, pouring tea into my cup.

"*Hope*. Humanity. Something worthy of my time and patience."

"You mean the selfish, illiterate oaf holds the key to the

universe?"

"No. I mean yes. Wait. Listen, please. He does hold the key in a way, but he isn't conscious of it. He's a diamond in the rough, Dooley. Like a character in one of those bad sci-fi movies you love so much, the ones where the protagonist is going to save the world but she doesn't know it yet."

"Ah. Our little girl is growing up. See how she wants to help the incredible shrivelled man? I mean *emotionally* shrivelled, by the way. I'm hoping he isn't hampered in more important areas."

"Can't you be serious for a moment, Dooley? I'm scared. I'm not sure of myself when I'm around Matthew. It's like I'm willing to fall twelve storeys for him. Not literally. Stop looking at me like that. No, I mean, have you ever had that dream where you are swimming around happily and then you start to go under and the sensation isn't frightening? It feels natural, as if you are going to sleep in the most peaceful way possible. As if you are going back to a place – a sensation – you remember. Going back to a universal memory perhaps, but, whatever it is, it feels like home."

Dooley was staring at me with her mouth open.

"OK, well, maybe it isn't that at all. Maybe it's lust, over-active hormones if you will. He is so very good-looking. Beautiful thick eyelashes and abs like a washboard."

"So I take it you two have . . ."

"No, not yet. But he's taking me to dinner and then we'll see," I said mysteriously.

"So, WHAT DO you want to know?" I said to her the following week over dim sum.

"Everything. Tell me everything."

"He's a great kisser."

"Come on, Elsa, get to the good stuff."

"It wasn't awkward and it wasn't amazing. It wasn't anything banal. I mean, I had wanted him so much, since I met him, but when we finally did it, I wasn't even thinking about his lips or smell, or how he felt pressed against me. When I closed my eyes and he touched me, it was . . ." I took a deep breath. "It was as if for the first time I began to understand my place in the universe."

"Wow," was all Dooley could say, leaning over in her chair so far I was afraid she would fall off. I had never seen her like this. My usually cool and collected friend seemed flushed, far too interested in one of my boyfriend stories, of which she had heard so many.

Our eyes met and I knew my intimate confession over tea had suddenly transcended everything: our friendship, our experiences, all the people we had ever loved. The walls of the Buddha seemed to pulsate with new energy, as if the restaurant was a generator and Dooley, Matt and I mere connections on a three-way plug. The electricity in the room could have lit a small village. Certainly that meant we were on to something special, right?

But I soon learned over the next few months that Matt was not the Starman with shiny constellations in his eyes that I'd hoped for. He was cold, insensitive and unable to be intimate on any level except physically. And even that wasn't as spectacular as I would have liked. Whatever hope I saw in him initially quickly faded to black, all but erased by the reality of his many shortcomings, like a fondness for Argyle socks in bed and memorising the names of fancy wines he had never tasted, just so he could sound knowledgeable at restaurants. Matt was neglectful of the bigger things, but pernickety about the little ones, becoming moody if he didn't book his regular appointments for facials, highlights, massages and wax jobs on his perfectly arched eyebrows. His beauty regime was so intense and complicated, he couldn't believe mine only included washing my face in the morning and occasionally remembering to moisturise. His little quirks, once so cute and unique, became intolerable, like needing to have CNN on in the background whenever we made love, Matt stopping whenever a news item caught his eye.

He seemed to detest everything I liked and felt jealous and insecure around my friends, whom he never wanted to meet. He forgot my birthday, didn't call when he said he would and showed up hours after we were supposed to meet. But none of it mattered in the end. I was determined to wait patiently until Matt's vulnerability made its appearance and his great ability to love me back was revealed.

I spent hours at the Buddha recounting his every word. Hope mixed with desire mixed with the excitement of always being on the edge of something that would eventually unfold. We dissected and carefully analysed my paramour's every action in the laboratory that was the Lucky Buddha, as if the answer to my obsession lay somewhere deep inside Matt's reluctance to love me.

Try as we might, we couldn't find the answers. Instead, I found it harder and harder to drag myself away from the relationship, even after I knew in my heart that I would never discover the secrets of the universe. I continued holding on to Matt as if he were a human life-raft and I was a sinking swimmer.

"How CAN I have fallen this hard for a jerk who doesn't think twice about hurting me?" I said to Dooley, three months later.

"I think you aren't giving him the benefit of the doubt, Elsa."

"You're kidding me, right? His flaws are like potholes."

"Don't be so negative. Think about what you can do to turn it around. There has to be something you can do to make Matthew respond. You have to get him to open up."

"OK, who are you and what have you done with my best friend's body?" I said, in a mock teen-horror voice. "Dooley, you are always the first to criticise my terrible taste in men. Remember Sanjo? He didn't even last two hours. I wasn't even through describing him and you'd already moved on to something else. So what gives?"

"I just think the worthy ones take more time. Why are you so eager to condemn him, Elsa?"

"Why are you so eager to defend him?"

We stared each other down. This had become more frequent in the last few weeks. The bickering and arguing and silences, sometimes so overwhelming I wondered how our friendship could ever survive.

"I want you to be happy. I want you to find a person who will keep you curious and alive. You're my closest friend and you know better than anyone that I'm not a mushy romantic, but I think Matthew may be the one, Elsa."

I searched her eyes for some sign of a joke, but she stared back with complete sincerity.

I didn't say anything, pretending to rummage in my handbag for money to share the bill. More and more I felt I couldn't share my real thoughts with Dooley. She was insistent on glossing over the problems in my relationship, almost as if she were the one making the decisions.

I finally came to terms with the impossibility of my relationship, having spent a weekend speed-dialling Matt's number, leaving message after desperate message, after the love of my life told me he was going back to his wife and children. A secret family he never bothered to mention. After I left one particularly unpleasant message, full of vitriol and bitterness, a soft-spoken woman answered the phone and with infinite calmness told me that her husband no longer wanted to speak to me and would I please stop calling.

After eight months of longing, waiting and wondering why

Matt wouldn't love me, I hit rock bottom.

Dooley called an emergency meeting at the Buddha.

I was in no mood to hear her I-am-woman-hear-me-roar or her Gloria Gaynor-cum-Destiny's Child I'm-a-survivor speech. I was hung-over, depressed and I hadn't slept in three days. But I desperately needed to talk to my friend. I was blown away when I heard what she had to say.

"So he has an inconvenient wife, big deal. Makes things more interesting. Spices it up a little, don't you think?"

"What? Have you been drinking the soy sauce, Dooley?"

"No, hear me out. We are close, so close, to figuring out what it is about this guy. I mean, how does he do it? How has he managed to hook us and hold us despite his, you know, *peccadilloes*."

"Peccadilloes?" I gave her a look over the plate of perpetual wontons. I couldn't believe she was defending him despite all our late-night chats – the hours spent talking about Matt's numerous and socially challenging shortcomings: like dandruff. "Matthew is bad news, Dooley. I don't want to spend another minute with him. You have no idea how stupid I feel. I should have realised he was married. I saw the signs and I ignored them, preferring to beat myself up instead."

"But they were estranged. Stop being so naïve and unsophisticated. He chose you, after all. The wife-and-kid thing is probably all about his guilt."

"That's not it. He is unavailable, Dooley. In the truest sense of the word. Wife or no wife. That he lied to me and didn't trust me enough to tell me he had kids just makes it worse."

"I'm sure he had his reasons."

"Yes, I'm sure he did, but I don't want to hang around long enough to find out what they are. I should be figuring out why I'm so attracted to men that treat me badly."

"So find out, but don't let go of Matthew. I think deep down inside he really loves you, Elsa."

I looked at her incredulously. "Look, I'm tired of you going on about it. This isn't a social experiment, Dooley. You are not Dr Frankenstein and this isn't some lab where you get to find out what love is composed of. This is my life. I love you, you're my best friend, but you can't continue hanging on to this doomed romance. I'm closing the door on this chapter."

Dooley, usually so thoughtful and protective of me, stared back at me coldly.

"I have spent week after week with you, listening to you complain, cry and talk about love and how it always manages to evade you. When you finally meet someone interesting, someone worthy, you let yourself be defeated by the first obstacle you come across. I'm just trying to help. Obviously, you don't need me." Putting some money down on the table, she rose and left the restaurant without another word.

I DIDN'T SEE Dooley for a few months after that. I decided to book some vacation time and stayed home, pigging out on junk food and watching television. I screened all my calls and refused to answer my door. Dooley didn't give up, of course. She started sending me emails. I even received the odd postcard or two – black-and-white stills from her favourite films. Not disaster movies, thankfully, although those would have been more fitting. One card she sent was of *Gone with the Wind* – the famous scene where Rhett carries Scarlett up the stairs. It said: "I know you are in avoidance mode, and that's fine. I'll be here when you are ready to stop being a hermit. Here are some movies to watch meanwhile: *When Harry Met Sally*; *Four Weddings and a Funeral*; *Titanic*; and *Pretty in Pink*. Actually, screw all that and watch *Blade*; Wesley Snipes is amazing."

None of the messages mentioned our last argument or Matt. I received a couple of emails from him as well, telling me how he was separating from his wife, this time for good.

And would I like to get together for dinner sometime to talk about things?

I didn't rejoice, nor did I feel vindicated. I didn't even keep the emails to savour again and again. I deleted them unceremoniously.

One day I received an unmarked package in brown paper. Inside was a book: *Intelligent Life in the Universe*, by Carl Sagan. There was a note on white card in handwriting I didn't recognise: "Humility and forgiveness are the proper paths to enlightenment. Don't let your narrow focus blind you to the beauty of the universe."

For a moment I was unsure if it was Matt or Dooley who had sent it. I kept the book, but deleted her emails as well.

After years of unconditional friendship, I realised that my best friend was fearless, except in situations that exposed her. Good old Dooley, who developed vertigo while *I* grappled with a mountain-sized version of self-hatred and insecurity; who stood beside me without caring for my emotional sanity, watching me fall and crumble in an undignified manner. Instead of pulling me to safety, she proposed to hurl me back across the unknown frontier like Laika the space dog, just to see what was on the other side.

She called that the enlightened path?

Over the next few solitary weeks, I began to do some serious thinking. Starting with my career. My dream had always been to write scripts, but for years I had been sucked into a soulless job, editing the work of other people. If I was to survive this mess and start living my life, I had to stop being so dependent on Dooley and others. I had to stand on my own.

I wrote myself a schedule and then stuck to it. Every morning I rose at 6:00 and jogged around the park near my house. I ran up and down the stairs of my apartment, forced myself to do chin-ups and taught myself t'ai chi with a video. I experimented with new recipes, read books I had neglected and, most importantly, I started writing again.

At first I felt a bit over the top, like Sylvester Stallone in *Rocky*, but with every new day I felt more and more confident and invincible. I wore my new attributes below the surface of my skin, comforted by the knowledge that I had secret skills no one else knew about. For now, it was enough for me to know they were there.

Ten weeks after my self-imposed confinement, I called Dooley to arrange a meeting at the Lucky Buddha. Sitting with a pot of jasmine tea between us, I felt as awkward as if I was on my first date.

"You look great, Elsa. All that time indoors would look frightful on most people. But you look healthy."

"Thanks."

"So, what did you do all that time?" she asked, pretending to look at the menu.

I didn't know why she bothered. Dooley always had the same thing: chicken kung pao, broccoli with garlic, tea, and white rice. Her order was as predictable as everything else in our relationship.

All of a sudden things were crystal clear. When I was with Dooley, nothing changed. I was still the same old person I was dying to leave behind. It was as if every unpleasant moment of humiliation and heartbreak of the last seven years was contained in the time capsule that was the Buddha.

Looking up from my chopsticks, I stared squarely into Dooley's eyes, those eyes that had measured my progress from past to present and were now preparing to hijack my future.

"I didn't do anything special. Not really," I said.

"Well, I'm glad you're back," she said with relief. "I missed you. So did Matthew."

She must have read the question in my eyes.

"I called him to see if he had heard from you. He said he

sent you a few emails, but you didn't bother emailing back."

"I didn't feel like writing, Dooley."

"Well, you're here now. Back where you belong. That's all that matters."

I stared at the plate of perpetual wontons.

"What's wrong? Aren't you hungry, El?"

"Don't you ever feel like going somewhere different? Do you realise this is the only place we've ever gone for dinner?"

"Hush, Mr Lee will hear you," whispered Dooley.

"Year after year we sit here and celebrate or commiserate. We dish up our lives like one of Mr Lee's main courses. And always to be shared between us. I am never a dish unto myself. Sometimes I think all I have of my own are a few fuzzy, imperfect moments when I'm not having conversations with you over tea."

"Just order some spring rolls and go home and get a good night's sleep. You obviously feel a bit flustered on your first day out," she snapped.

"It's not that simple. I wish it were. I'm twenty-nine years old, Dooley. Twenty-nine and I feel time is already standing still."

"Stop being so melodramatic, Elsa. What are you *really* saying? That your life is boring? That your friendship with me, all this" – she gestured around the room at the cracking leatherette booths – "everything we share is insignificant because you haven't experienced it alone? Do you realise how hopelessly *bourgeois* you sound? Some people would give anything to stem the loneliness. Do you hear me? They would give anything to share their lives with someone, just for a few hours."

I looked down at my hands. I knew Dooley would approach it rationally. But I was sick of logic; I wanted to experience random moments. I didn't want the dress rehearsal, the rehashing of possibilities in the safety of the Buddha's womb. I wanted adventure and excitement and the opportunity to be surprised.

"You just don't get it," I finally said, putting down my chopsticks.

"How can I understand when you don't talk, Elsa? You've been uncommunicative for months. First I thought it was because of what's-his-name. But then I realised it wasn't. It's about us, isn't it? You are angry at me."

"I'm going away, Dooley, to Peru. I answered an ad for an Italian crew looking for an assistant. They are filming a documentary of Machu Picchu. I'll be gone for months. I'm not sure when I'll be back. I'm leaving next week."

She put down her teacup. "Why didn't you tell me before?" she said in a quiet voice. "I'm your best friend and you didn't bother telling me till now?"

"I don't know, Dooley. It was very sudden."

"So let me get this straight. You are going to South America indefinitely, to work on a vague project having to do with mountains. But you waited till now to tell me? What do you want from me? A blessing?"

"I want you to understand."

"Well, I'm finding it a little hard. Look, we all have our fantasies. I am queen of fantasy land. But don't confuse fantasy with reality. I think about going away sometimes, but my life is here with you and my friends. There is nowhere I'd rather be. Do you think running away will solve your problems? Is that it? This isn't a movie of the week, goddamn you."

"This is exactly why I need to go. I feel stifled, Dooley, I can't continue to live my life by your observations. I am an outsider in my own world. I can't continue eating wontons and drinking tea at the Buddha until both of us are too old and useless to do anything else but tell each other stories."

"OK. I get it. You are an adult. You want to be alone? Fine. I don't need you to tell me any more. I understand."

There was nothing now but silence between us. Silence and those fucking stale, wretched wontons.

I thought about all the things we had survived, all the exes and the excesses and the doubts and self-mutilation of women who were constantly analysing the questions as well as the answers to their lives.

"I'm sorry, but I have to do this. I need to make mistakes. We have been friends for a long time, Dooley, I hope –"

She held up a hand.

I looked up expecting to see her red-traffic-light eyes, but Dooley was crying quietly into the plate of wontons.

Solomon's Call

My father, Edgar Chevere, came home from work one day clutching a flyer. "What do you think of this?" he asked in Spanish, shoving the piece of paper into my mother's face.

"'Are you a lover of expressionism? A devotee of imaginative, inspirational theatre?'" she read. "'If you are a talented actor who fits this description, the Hallford Acting and Musical Society would like to hear from you. Auditions: Tuesday, 7:00.'"

"Can you believe it? Experimental theatre right here in Hallford. I better start rehearsing right away."

"You're not serious, Pops?" I said. "You're going to try out for a group called the HAMS? Get real."

"Leave your father alone, Ophelia," said my mother, her lips twitching.

That evening we watched as he practised rabbit-gnawing motions in the bathroom mirror.

"Your father knows what he is doing. Did you know that in our country he used to teach drama?"

Edgar puffed out his puny chest. "When I was younger

man, I was bestest actor of all," he said in his broken English. "Now, not so bestest any more."

"Best," I said from the doorway. "Not bestest, Dad. *Best*."

I WAS NINE when my mother and I moved to New York. My mother knew English, having learned as a little girl, but I struggled to fit in.

"Why can't we go back home to Ecuador?" I kept asking. "Why did we come here?"

"Things are not so good in our country. When they get better, we will return. Until then, you will have to try harder, Ophelia."

"What about Dad? Why isn't he here with us?"

"Your father will join us soon. Now, come on. Don't cry. It will be fine."

But it wasn't. Everything was strange and foreign. I was enrolled in a new school and spent the first year not speaking. On the few occasions when I'd tried to answer my teacher's questions, something happened to my lips: they moved, but no sound came out. The kids at school made jokes, flapping their hands as if I had gills.

"Fish Face. La Fishy. Hey, Goldfish," they called out.

Father remained in Guayaquil, unaware of my troubles. Once a month he called and told us how much he missed us.

"When are you coming, Dad?" I asked, trying not to make my voice too obvious.

"Soon, Ophelia," he promised. "Now put your mother back on."

It took him five years.

When he finally arrived, he carried one battered suitcase in one hand and a misshapen teddy bear in the other. We met him at the airport dressed in our Sunday clothes. Mother had sent Edgar photos over the years, but he still stared in confusion as we greeted him at the gate.

"But you are practically a woman," he said. "Not even a little girl any more." He shoved the twisted teddy into my arms.

Not knowing what to do, I picked at its glassy eyes. The thread came loose and one of them fell to the floor.

Edgar frowned and then burst into tears.

"*Ophelia,*" said my mother.

I had somehow imagined the reunion with my father to be more dignified. I found it difficult to believe that the teary, dark, skinny man standing before me was really who he said he was. I'd pictured him much taller.

On the bus ride home, Edgar kept up the theatrics, touching my mother's arm, stroking her hair and whispering in Spanish. Mother wore the same tight face she wore whenever she came to parents' evening at my school.

"Why doesn't he speak English?" I asked loudly, noticing that other passengers on the bus were staring. "Everyone here speaks English."

"Leave your father alone, Ophelia."

"Give the girl time, Dora," said my father.

"I think that's the problem, Edgar. She's had too much time."

No one said anything after that.

I turned towards the window and focused on a tiny ant making its patient way across the pane, struggling with a piece of bread three times its size. Its pathetic journey suddenly irritated me. Before it reached its destination, I squished it neatly with the palm of my hand.

AFTER HE MOVED back in with us, my father began looking for

a job. It didn't help that he always referred to English as the "enemy" tongue and never bothered to learn it properly.

"Why do I need it?" he said to my mother, after another batch of résumés proved unsuccessful. "This language is such a harsh one, cold and inexpressive. Good for business, yes. But not for speaking."

"We talked about this, Edgar. Speaking Spanish will not help you in this country."

"But Castellano is the language of romance, of Don Quixote, poets and kings."

"Ay. How many times have I told you? In *America*, Spanish is the language of the penniless immigrant. If you want a job, you must learn to speak the *gringo* tongue."

AT MY MOTHER's insistence, my father signed up with an agency that specialised in helping people like him. He paid a hefty fee just to hear what he already knew: that the labour market was saturated with thousands of Latin Americans fleeing from tyrants, loons, despots, collapsing economies and ex-guerrillas turned president.

"Take Ophelia along to translate," said my mother. So I was allowed the day off school to go downtown with him.

"Señor Chevere, it is difficult to find employment at the moment. Everyone is competing for the same handful of entry-level jobs," said Ms Estepona, his caseworker.

"Entry level? There must be some misunderstanding. I am a learned man. I have a doctorate. I have teaching experience. Surely there is need for education in this country?"

"Do you have any idea how many immigrants have pedigrees like yours? It makes no difference. I'm afraid you have no choice but to learn the language. Then you can be assured we will find you something."

"Can you guarantee it will be in my field?"

The caseworker regarded my father with dead eyes.

"I'm afraid you *still* don't understand. You are no longer in *Latin* America. You cannot move here and expect preferential treatment."

"No, no. I don't want special treatment. I want to find a job!"

"Do not raise your voice at me," the caseworker said, putting her long nails in my father's face. He shrank back.

"Look, my dad just needs to find a job," I said. "Don't you have anything he can do?"

"If he wants to provide for his family," she said, barely glancing at me, "he is going to have to forget everything and start over again. Look, I don't make the rules. That's how it is. I'm afraid there's nothing more we can offer him."

"Ask her about *her* job," my father said to me. "I could do that quite easily. Even with my atrocious English, it would be a vast improvement on her so-called bilingualism."

"Tell your father to learn the language or go back to Ecuador," said Ms Estepona, calling out the next number. My father picked up the folder holding his important papers and shuffled out, signalling me to follow.

"Those people are predators, preying on the weak. I'll get a job on my own, you will see."

BUT AFTER SIX months he was still unable to find anyone who wanted to hire him. He sat day after day watching television and circling job ads, waiting for someone to return his calls. At first he was picky, telling us he would only accept office jobs that required him to wear a jacket: maybe in a bank or an academic position. When that didn't pan out, he modified his requirements to include outdoor jobs: construction or overseeing road works, although he wasn't really the outdoorsy type. Finally Edgar said he would take anything that came along. Just for the time being, you understand.

His first job was as a pizza delivery man. Since we didn't own a car, Edgar had to deliver the pizzas on an old bicycle. Then he was a flower delivery "boy" at the local florist. After that, he worked as a dishwasher at a diner. That one only lasted a week.

He eventually obtained a position as custodian at the local community college. The hours were long and solitary and the role didn't require my father to speak, but at least he felt comfortable in the familiarity of his old environment as he mopped and buffed the classroom floors.

"FOR THE HAMS audition, I've chosen a classical piece," Edgar said, sitting us down on the living-room couch. "Tell me what you think.

"'O what a drudge and sport of Gods am I!'" he recited, his hand over his chest for effect. "'Of whose ill plight no whisper ever came To my own home, or any coast of Greece ...'"

I was surprised at my father's delivery; being only fourteen, I had not yet discovered the Greek tragedies and it was the first time I had seen him perform. This previously silent man suddenly came to life; his black eyes blazed and even his boots crackled with energy.

"You don't think *Philoctetes* is too much?"

"I think it shows how learned you are," said my mother.

"What if they don't understand?"

"A good actor should be able to transcend the language barrier."

"You are right, of course. You are always right. But what if they want a contemporary piece instead?"

"Then do something from *Taxi Driver*. You've memorised every line, Edgar."

"Wha' do ju tink of dis?"

I rolled my eyes. I had not been allowed to see *Taxi Driver*, but I was certain Robert De Niro hadn't sounded anything like my father.

After he rushed off to the audition, my mother told me that back in Guayaquil, when he was younger, my father had been an award-winning orator and poet.

"It's been difficult for Edgar to find his feet in this country. It is good that he's trying out for these HUMPS."

"HAMS," I said. "And what's so special about reading poems to a roomful of strangers? In our English class, Mrs Monroe makes us do it all the time. And if Dad was such a big shot, why is he cleaning floors now?"

"Ay, what a thing to say, Ophelia! Please, have a little respect. You may not believe it, but there is more to him than meets the eye. Your father is an *artist*, an *eccentric*, and an *extrovert*." She pronounced each word reverently.

Despite what she said, I knew my father wasn't really an artist. Artists wore nice clothes and had lots of money. They went to fancy parties and hung out with famous people. My father owned one suit we purchased at the Sears, Roebuck outlet. Plus, he didn't know anyone except Mr and Mrs Sanchez from down the hall, and they didn't count. And Dad wasn't an extrovert. He wore an ugly blue uniform and bowed his head like a subservient donkey whenever anyone said something he didn't understand.

For the millionth time I wished I had a father who was a policeman or a teacher: something more interesting than just a floor cleaner who couldn't speak the language.

"I hope I never end up like him. I hope I never turn out to be a janitor."

"A custodian. Not a janitor. Your father is a *custodian*. And be careful what you wish for."

AFTER THE AUDITION, my father came home silent and tired. Despite my mother's prompts he said little. She warmed up his food and sat on the opposite side of the table watching him eat.

"Did everything go well?"

He shook his head.

"Did you do *Philoctetes*?"

He shook his head again.

"*Antigone*?"

My father stopped eating.

"Edgar, please tell me what happened."

"They couldn't understand my De Niro," he said, his dark eyes moist.

"Not understand? But it was perfect: the accent, the mannerisms . . ."

My father pushed his plate away. "I don't want to talk about it. I'm going to bed, Dora."

My mother took me aside and forbade me to mention the failed audition. In fact, I was not to mention the words play, actor, drama or ham around my father.

Edgar brooded around the house, quieter than usual, until one evening, when he came in banging the front door.

"Guess what?" he said excitedly. "Miss Dixon, the director of HAMS, called me at work today. She wants me to come to their next rehearsal!"

"That's wonderful, Edgar."

"Yeah, that's great, Pops."

"I won't get any parts at first, but Miss Dixon said I showed promise. She said I had style, grace and charisma. She said I reminded her of a young Omar Sharif." My father smiled at us with all his teeth. "I must go and practise," he said, locking himself in the bathroom.

Rehearsals were on Tuesdays and Thursdays. Edgar came home exhausted but happy to his reheated dinners. At the kitchen table, he recounted the events of the evening, telling of Miss Dixon's latest crazy idea or describing the lighting and costumes for the set. Between bites, he told us who forgot their lines, who was carrying on with whom and who was hamming it up on the floorboards. That was the thing my father loved the most: introducing us to phrases like "hamming it up on the floorboards".

"So, when will you have a chance to 'thread the boards'?" I asked after it had been going on for some time. "When is Miss Dixon finally going to give you a part?"

"Patience, Ophelia," said my father. "My time will come."

Seven months later, he still hadn't landed a role. Not even a minor one. He didn't seem too bothered, however. He was content to hang out with the players, helping them rehearse their lines, building scenery and whatever else needed doing. My father was so grateful they wanted him; he would have swept the floors if they'd asked.

"DORA, OPHELIA, I have great news," he said to us one day over dinner. "Miss Dixon took me aside again. You will never guess – she's asked me to write a play. *In English*! And I will also act in it. Isn't that fantastic? I am not only actor, I am playwright." He beamed at us from across the table.

We were too stunned to reply.

Previously my father had been so conscious of his heavy accent that he refused to say even "please" and "thank you". Now he was going to write and act in front of other people?

"Aren't you happy for me, Dorita?" he asked with soft eyes.

"Of course," she said.

But I could tell her heart wasn't really in it.

MY FATHER TURNED into a real actor after that. Before his play, he'd come home tired from his job and fall asleep on the couch in front of the television. Now in the evenings he jumped into the bathroom and out again, transformed like a superhero.

"Waddya think? Do I look *cool*? Gimme some skin."

With his curly hair no longer neatly combed to the side and wearing a black turtleneck and tight flared trousers, my father resembled a shorter, hairier Latino version of Isaac Hayes in *Shaft*.

"Dy-no-mite" was his new favourite saying, as well as "sock it to me", said with his hand palm-side up.

My mother was less than pleased with these new developments.

"Tell me you aren't going to rehearsals dressed like that," she said.

"Why, what's wrong with the way I'm dressed?"

"Edgar," she said, staring at the tight trousers. "It isn't exactly suitable. Why don't you wear your blue suit?"

"I can't breathe in that suit. This is more comfortable. More me," he said, splashing Old Spice on the thin goatee he was attempting to grow. "Besides, everyone at HAMS wears jeans, Dora. No one wears suits. Don't be uptight mama. It ain't cool."

"I wasn't aware you had to be like everyone else to fit in," said my mother.

"I had a vision the other night."

"What, like Joan of Arc?" I said innocently from the table where I was doing my homework.

"I realised my true calling was never to teach, Dora. I was destined to write, perhaps even direct some day."

"But we talked about this, Edgar. You're going to take night classes and get certified. Acting is nice, but it isn't going to pay the bills."

"The world doesn't need another teacher. It needs another Martin Scoretski."

"Don't be ridiculous, Edgar," she snapped.

"Scorsese," I said.

"*Que*?"

"It's Martin *Scorsese*. You know? The guy who did *Taxi Driver*."

"Yes, Scoretski, that's what I said."

IT TOOK HIM six months to write his first draft. Father may have composed poetry in his youth, but it had been years since he'd written anything new and certainly never in the "enemy tongue". I'd never seen anyone put in as much effort as he did into that script. After work, he adjourned to the living room with a dictionary and one of my old school notebooks, a pencil behind each ear, pacing and talking to himself; scribbling and scratching out words and clutching at his hair.

Sometimes he would ask about certain phrases he overheard on the TV.

"What means 'you gotta go with the flow'?"

"You know, just like to be *cool*, relaxed, laid back. You know, hang out."

He gave me a quizzical look.

"You have to stop worrying so much, Dad. Go with the flow means you let things happen naturally, without forcing them."

"Ah. I think I understand. Back in Guayaquil when I was young, I was – how you say? – *flowing* all the time."

"Laid back, you mean."

"Yes. I never worried about the next day. A simple man is the happiest man. Do you know that saying?"

I shook my head.

"When you get older, Ophelia, and you start having responsibilities, you stop being laid back. You worry about everything. The world becomes a dangerous place."

He sat on the couch, pencil poised in mid air. "Like the great Solomon. He was wisest man of all. Given all knowledge and secrets of universe, but it made him unhappy. All he wanted to do was dance and sing, not be king."

"What's your play about, Dad?"

"It is a surprise. Sufficient to say it was inspired by *Jesus Christ Superstar*."

Dad had taken Mom to watch *Superstar* at the Luna three times. Mother told me that at the end of the film, my father had burst into tears, telling everyone within hearing distance that it was proof that serious musical theatre was possible.

"I hope Miss Dixon likes the play," he said, making notes in his book.

"How about Mom? Do you think she will like it?"

My father gave me an odd look. "Ophelia, when an artist has a vision, sometimes those closest to him are the ones that understand the least. Do you understand?"

I didn't. I had no idea what he was on about.

ONE EVENING WHILE we were having dinner, Miss Dixon called. My mother silently passed the phone to my father.

"Let's talk tomorrow. I must eat with my family now. Yes, I see. Of course."

"What does she want, Edgar?"

"She wants to talk about the play," he said, wiping his mouth and pushing his plate away.

"Can't it wait until tomorrow?"

"She needs to speak to me now."

"But you haven't finished your dinner!"

"Tell her to leave you alone. That's what Scorsese would do," I said, my mouth full of mashed potatoes.

"Ophelia, please, mind your manners."

"If she's being demanding, quit, Dad."

"No, don't you see? I have to finish. I am a professional. I am not a prima donna." His voice rose at the edges.

My mother picked up a plate of peas and for a moment I thought she was going to hurl them at him. "So the *gringa* gets her way?" she said.

"This isn't about her, this is about me. Do you want me to quit too, Dora? Is that it? You want me to clean floors all day? Stay here and watch television with you every night? Listen," he said, indicating with a finger the space where his two brows met, "I am a smart man. Back in Ecuador I was something. Here I am nothing. But now I have a chance to write a play. Miss Dixon believes in me. All the HAMS believes. Everyone, except my own family." He got up from the table, gathered his notebooks and firmly shut the front door behind him.

"Mom, is it true that Dad stayed behind in Ecuador because –"

"Not now, Ophelia."

"But he said –"

"I said not now."

OVER THE NEXT few weeks, my father barely spoke to us. He came home, changed out of his uniform, moved my mother's porcelain figurines out of harm's way and spent his nights prancing around our living room in his underpants. He repeated his lines in front of the bathroom mirror over and over again, sometimes in English, sometimes in Spanish and most of the time in a made-up gibberish language in between. A few times I even saw him succumb to tears on our living-room couch, overcome by the emotion of his own performance. Sometimes in the mornings, before school, I'd find him in his clothes sprawled out on the floor, surrounded by balled-up pieces of paper, looking like a drunk I once saw in the park.

EDGAR'S PLAY DEBUTED on Easter Sunday. The stage was decorated with spring flowers and every seat was filled. Miss Dixon stood at the front wearing a soft-pink outfit. She made a little speech and then proudly introduced *Solomon's Call*, which she referred to as "an experimental musical monologue".

The curtains went up and my father appeared in the shadows, anguish apparent on his countenance as he knelt in supplication in the two inches of wet playground sand he'd asked me to collect for him. Miss Dixon's disembodied voice recounted Solomon's early life in the desert, describing in effusive tones how the young king heard God's voice, understanding in the blink of an eye how the sun was able to rise above his head. To demonstrate this enlightenment, one of the HAMS in charge of special effects shone a spotlight directly into my father's eyes, nearly blinding him. Someone cued a disco number and Edgar, wearing nothing but a handkerchief-sized loincloth and copious amounts of Johnson's baby oil, stumbled across the stage like a sailor on a three-day bender.

"And Solomon danced," yelled Miss Dixon loudly from the wings, and my father began to jump and writhe to the beat of the music as if possessed by demons.

While I had seen him stretching and leaping over furniture at home, I was completely unprepared for the shock of seeing my father perform. I sat stunned, third row from the back, praying that he didn't trip over his own feet and land sprawled sunny-side up on centre stage.

Edgar's figure did not possess the anorexic elegance of a Nureyev, nor did he have any classical training, yet he still managed to keep his audience riveted. We watched as Solomon danced across his kingdom, pirouetting and flying through the air, the beads of sweat and baby oil highlighting his knotty calves. On stage, he appeared taller and larger than in real life, his physique kept trim by a regime of sweeping floors and acrobatics in our living room.

The final number in my father's piece, the scene he'd mystically named "Three", called for even more passionate kneeling and leaping than the scenes before. Edgar utilised every part of his body to emote; even his hips acted – fast wiggle meant turbulence in the kingdom, slow sway was peace and unity with God. But as the pace grew more and more frenetic, my father started tiring, panting, and even stopping in the middle of one of his numbers to catch his breath, looking more like ageing Puck than wise King of Israel.

I soon stopped trying to figure out the meaning behind *Solomon's Call*. As the story reached its climax, my father performed an outlandish and bizarre version of the whirling dervish, battling with all his might against the forces of time and gravity, even as the insignificance of his apparel began to make itself felt.

When the great king finally dropped to his knees to offer heartfelt thanks to his God, he was not alone. As the sun set on the wisest of all wise men, the audience let out a deep and relieved breath.

Edgar's leg, however, must have cramped up from the dancing. As he tried to leap up for the much trumpeted "call", Solomon tripped and the magical thread holding his loincloth snapped.

My father was revealed on stage in all his glory.

The gasps of the congregation threatened to overpower the disco music and someone, possibly one of his fellow HAMS, cried out, "Oh dear God, I can see Solomon's balls!"

My father quickly recovered, pausing long enough to glare out over the audience until there was a complete and hushed silence. Waiting for the narration from Miss Dixon, which never came, he stood before us, ever the consummate professional, lifted his hands high above his head and said in perfect, clear English, "And Solomon, like King David, danced naked before the Lord."

Those not frozen from shock either coughed or tittered, while I tried to hold back my tears. Thankfully, the number was short. Edgar threw himself to the ground one last time, lowered his head and waited for the applause. Hearing nothing but a collective intake of breath, my father, with the little dignity he had left, stood up, recovered his torn loincloth and exited stage left.

The murmurs started almost immediately.

"Well I never . . . I cannot believe . . . goes to show what you get . . ."

Miss Dixon's pretty face was flushed. "Please, everyone, just calm down."

I turned to look at my mother. But instead of the anger or the humiliation I'd imagined, there were tears running down her face.

"Bravo," she said. "Bravo."

A few of the more progressive HAMS joined in. "Bravo, Edgar, bravo!"

The audience stopped whispering and stared uncertainly, wondering if they had missed anything.

My father, dressed in a robe, came shyly out from the wings. He exchanged a look with Miss Dixon and then searched the sea of faces in the audience until he found us.

The silent janitor shrank in the shadow of this new man, the unapologetic exhibitionist, who had pranced, growled, jumped and thrown himself with every ounce of energy across the boards. My father stared at me expectantly.

"Way to go, Dad," I said loudly, standing up and stomping my feet. "*Dy-no-mite.*"

THE SHED

HENRY HAMPSTEAD WAS just eight weeks into his retirement and already he was driving his wife crazy.

He came in from the garden, stomping his muddy boots on the chenille carpet and blowing on his hands. "It's bloody freezing out there. Any chance of a cuppa?"

"I thought you were using the space heater," replied Carla, without looking up from her book.

Henry shook his head. "The heater gives me a headache."

"Why do you want to work in the shed anyway? It's cold and damp and full of spiders. Especially when I set up that nice new computer for you in the spare room."

"I can't *write* on that, I already told you." He sat down on the couch beside her. "Everything is too tidy. Computers are for keeping track of budgets and spreadsheets, not writing. That's what typewriters are for. Plus, I *like* the shed. Dylan Thomas worked in his shed, you know. Did some of his best writing there."

"Dylan Thomas had enough ethanol in his blood to keep him warm. You're going to catch your death out there." Carla took one of his hands in hers and rubbed it gently. "If you are going to insist on working outside, can't you at least wear a warm sweater and a pair of gloves?"

"Remind me after supper," he said, unlacing his boots and resting his head against the worn upholstery of the settee.

"You're going out again?"

"I am just getting started, Carla. I'm not an automaton, you know. These things take time. I'll get the hang of it soon enough. You know what they say about persistence . . ."

"Well, your stubborn persistence is going to give you pneumonia," she said, heading towards the kitchen.

"Any chance you can make it a strong black coffee instead of tea?"

"You know what the doctor said, Henry. Coffee isn't good for your blood pressure. But, if you're nice, maybe I'll let you have a few biscuits."

"Please tell me we're having the shortbread ones. You know how much I like those. Or oatmeal, the chewy ones with sultanas." Henry rubbed his hands together in anticipation. "Anything but ginger nut."

Carla brought in a tray with two steaming mugs. "I'm afraid that's all we have."

He glared at the offending biscuits. "I don't know why we always have to have the same old things. Why can't we try something different?"

"But you love ginger nut!"

"*Used* to. A man is allowed to change, isn't he?"

"So, don't eat them. *I* still like them."

"Well, don't take them away. I didn't say I wouldn't eat them." He held on to the plate with both hands. "I'd just like something new now and then." Henry stuffed two biscuits into his mouth and mimed the ups and downs of life's changes and how important it was to turn over new leaves. "Keep them guessing, that's my motto, Carla. Always keep the reader guessing. Once you become predictable, it's all over. No point going on any more," he said, with his mouth full.

Carla sighed. She wondered if this was his way of telling her she had become boring. She hadn't really been paying attention because she was trying to catch the crumbs Henry was spilling on the carpet.

"Well, I'm heading back out," he said. "I'll be in my *office* if you need me."

"But your supper . . . you said you were going out later."

"I'm not hungry any more."

"But I made your favourite: lamb stew with peas."

"Leave it in the oven, Carla. It will save."

He put on his boots, took two more biscuits from the plate and before she could utter a word in protest, he was gone.

IN HIS LAST few months as office manager at the paper mill, Henry had taken to making long, extravagant lists of potential occupations he could take up once he retired. Handy man, landscape painter and crossword-puzzle contributor were all favourite choices, handwritten in fluorescent ink, underlined and placed on Post-it notes around his office and home. Topping the list week after week was *writer*.

More than anything, Henry wanted to write.

"No need to go on holiday the way Bob Connelly did," he said to his wife at the local Harvester, where he'd taken her for a celebration meal. "Booked a cruise to South Asia for two months and gained a stone from all that rich food. Me, I couldn't take it. I prefer to be productive. Nurture my creative nature."

Carla cut her meat into neat, careful pieces. "It wouldn't be a bad thing if we went somewhere together, Henry. Just a few days – doesn't have to be anywhere fancy. A little holiday

– just the two of us. We could visit your sister Edna. You love the Lake District. Spend the days taking long walks and talking – the way we used to. Then when we return, you can start your writing in earnest."

"No," he said, his mouth full of potatoes. "No. The time is *now*. You know what they say, 'Strike while the iron is hot.'"

For a retirement gift, Carla had bought him a matching burgundy-leather desk set of famous literary quotes, accompanied by a motivational book called *365 Phrases to Success*. Henry copied these sayings faithfully on to coloured bits of paper and scattered them throughout the house. "Better late than never" was taped to the refrigerator. "Carpe diem" was on the bathroom wall upstairs. "The early bird catches the worm" was under the telephone. Carla wasn't allowed to remove them, so she wiped and dusted around the Post-its. But now and then she swapped them around a little, just to see if Henry would notice.

Carla had retired three years previously, after working for almost two decades as a dental assistant. Now that the children were grown, she found plenty of things to occupy her free time. She joined a book club, enrolled in drawing classes at the college, and volunteered at a local charity shop. She looked forward to Henry's retirement, anticipating all the things they would do together. She wrote out a list of potential projects: gardening, pottery, an over-50s theatre group, Italian lessons, salsa dancing, even Thai cooking classes. Henry took one look at Carla's list and told her he wasn't interested. He certainly wasn't about to waste his precious time on stupid pots and plants, much less learning to dance for her benefit. He wanted to write and that was the only thing he wanted to do.

"I don't see the point of these activities. And you should keep some days free in case I need help. If I start publishing my work, I'm going to be far too busy to do everything myself."

"Do you really think it will get that far, Henry?" Carla asked, buttering a piece of bread.

"Why, don't you think I have what it takes?"

"I don't know. I don't know a thing about how books are published."

He put down his fork and looked at her, wounded.

"I mean, of course I have *faith* in you, Henry. I know if you put your mind to it you can do anything."

Carla reached out and put her hand on top of his.

"Good, it's settled then," he said, gently withdrawing his hand. "I knew I could count on you." Henry pushed his chair back from the table and, after giving her a dry peck on the cheek, went back to his writing.

So Carla Hampstead – mother, wife, retiree and budding watercolour artist, voted Most Efficient Employee of the Year nine times running – now spent her free days tidying the house, reading recipes and waiting for her husband to come in from the shed.

IT HAD STARTED raining; winter wrestling with spring, the skies constantly grey with heavy storm clouds.

"Do you have to chew so loudly?" Henry asked his wife. He was in a dour mood, watching from the kitchen window as the fat drops beat down on the garden.

"I'm not chewing loudly," said Carla.

"I can hardly hear myself think."

"Well, I'm eating the way I always do. I'll chew more softly, if that will help." She nibbled at the edges of her toast, trying not to make a sound, but once she became conscious of her teeth, she found it difficult to stop herself from chewing more loudly.

"The shed is leaking," Henry announced. "I noticed it yesterday. It's a small leak, but we'd better have someone in to fix it before it gets worse. I would do it myself, but I'm at a crucial part of my story. I can't afford to stop now..."

"Better not. Especially with your bad back."

"If we don't get someone in, the hole will grow and pretty soon the whole roof will cave in."

"I'll phone around. I think Thelma's husband does handy work. I'll ask if he's available."

"Good," he said, turning back to the window.

"Henry, what's your story about?"

"I'm afraid I can't really talk about it. I don't want to spoil it."

"But you'll tell me later, when you're ready?"

"Yes, of course. I have to get back to work now."

She watched through the window as her husband disappeared into the garden.

She wondered why he was always so secretive about his writing. The one time she had visited him in the shed, she was taking him a freshly baked pie. She thought he would enjoy the surprise, but curiosity overtook her and instead of knocking on the door, she peeked in at the little window to see what he was up to.

She could see his ordered desk with the old Corona typewriter and the two dozen very sharp pencils he kept in a soup tin on his desk. Sharpening made him concentrate, he said. Every morning before he did anything else, Henry sharpened his pencils and arranged his ruled notepads into neat little piles.

But he was not sitting in his leather chair that afternoon. He was pacing the length of the room, gnawing on the end of a pencil and wearing a tri-corner hat and eye patch.

Henry had looked up to see his wife of thirty-two years, staring at him through the shed window in open-mouthed wonder and he'd been so outraged that he ran at her, screaming and cussing like a demented pirate.

Carla dropped the pie and fled the garden in a flood of

tears.

Although he apologised later, she hadn't been out to the shed since.

"I need curtains," he said to her one evening, while they were in bed.

"What on earth for?"

"I like to feel protected. I was thinking maybe the shed could do with one of those black pull shades photographers use."

"I said I wouldn't bother you any more, Henry."

"I know. It isn't that. I just feel happier knowing I won't be interrupted. Also, it will block out that annoying rain."

"But you have little light as it is. You'll strain your eyes."

"I'll take in some table lamps. That will make the room cosier."

"But the spare room has a big window. Plenty of natural light – good for writing."

"I write better in the dark," he said. "Some of the best poets and writers wrote in darkness, with just a candle for company. Maybe I should write by candlelight. It's difficult to concentrate when there's too much light. You think you can find me some spare fabric to make the curtains?"

Carla didn't answer.

"Are you awake?" he said, shaking her shoulder. "Look, if you buy me the material, I'll make my *own* curtains."

Make his own? Henry couldn't make a cup of tea by himself.

"I'll run them up for you," she offered, turning towards him. "I have just the perfect pattern in mind, too."

"Now don't go getting all excited. I don't want anything frilly or flowery," he said, "just dark curtains. Like you find in a bachelor pad."

So that was it . . . No wonder he spent all his time in the shed alone, dressing up in strange outfits; he was daydreaming about what it was like to be single! Was this what they meant by a mid-life crisis? Carla wondered if a leggy blonde and the inevitable red sports convertible were next. She turned on to her side, hoping that was the end of the curtain conversation. Sometimes she felt the longer she knew her husband, the less she knew him.

A few days later, as she was looking through her mail-order catalogues and decorating pages for Henry's curtains, she ran across an advert in the back of a magazine:

```
            WANTED: NEW WRITERS
Feeling  unchallenged  and  unsatisfied?
Dream  of  doing  something  different?
We're  looking  for  stories  for  our
writing  magazine:  romance,  mystery,
sci-fi - we accept any genre.

    1st prize: £100 & publication

      2nd prize: £25 & 5 copies
            of the magazine

    Top 10 entries receive a Blue
     Mosquito Secrets of Writing
      book with accompanying DVD
```

Carla cut out the page carefully with her shearing scissors and tacked it to the refrigerator so Henry would find it when he came in from writing.

"What's this?" he asked, putting the milk on the counter.

"Isn't it just perfect? I found it in last month's *Home and Garden*. If you win you get to be in the magazine. Imagine that – your story *published*, Henry. At the very least you could win the writing book and DVD."

Henry inhaled deeply and held it closer with trembling hands.

"Rubbish," he pronounced. "Absolute rubbish. I'm not going to submit my story to this place."

"Why ever not?"

"I just can't, Carla. If I send them my story, how do I know they won't steal my ideas? No, it's too risky. You don't write, so I can't expect you to understand, but it's not just putting words down on paper. It's a lot of hard work. Things don't always fit the way you want them to." He crumpled the advert into a ball, tossed it in the bin and stormed out of the kitchen without another word.

Carla waited until she heard the back door slam before fishing out the page with a pencil. After wiping off a bit of leftover carrot on one corner, she smoothed it out and tucked it away neatly in her sewing basket.

Eventually, when he was ready, he would be glad she'd saved the clipping for him.

But as Carla went around the house doing her daily chores, she found that the silly little advert had stayed with her.

Dream of doing something different?

Carla would stop whatever she was doing, retrieve it from her basket and sigh. She must have read it a hundred times and each time it was like an incantation. She even started having dreams about it. One night, she was awarded a golden trophy in the shape of an insect and pronounced Blue Mosquito Writer of the Year. "But I'm not even a writer," said dream-Carla, clutching the award close to her chest.

"HAVE YOU CALLED someone about the shed?" asked Henry. It was mid April now and the rain would not stop falling.

"No. Not yet. It slipped my mind. I'm sorry."

"Make sure you don't forget. The wood is rotting and I've counted at least three leaks. Fortunately, they're in minor places. We might need to replace the entire thing, just the same. What's for lunch?" he asked, lifting lids off the pots.

"I made some vegetable soup."

"No meat?"

"No, but we have green beans and new-potato salad."

"Carla . . . I'm tired of soups and salads. I told you, I prefer sandwiches: meat, cheese, lots of pickle and mustard. Is that so hard to remember?"

"You know what the doctor said . . ."

"To hell with the doctor!" Henry slammed his hand down on the counter. "It's always 'The doctor said this, the doctor said that.' Let me have some pleasures, woman!"

Carla continued flipping through *100 Heart-Friendly Recipes*, as if he hadn't said a word. He turned abruptly to rummage in the broom cupboard until he found a bucket, a dustpan, a handful of clothes-pegs and a mop.

Henry was getting peculiar. She'd read about this. How some men who had worked their entire lives didn't know how to act when they had time on their hands. At first Carla was glad Henry was writing; it was a good hobby and it kept him occupied. But even this had turned awkward. He had become sullen and demanding, temperamental and hard to please. With Carla treading on eggshells, second-guessing his wishes, who could blame her for forgetting about the shed? In any event, in a few weeks the problem took care of itself, the rain stopping altogether.

Summer bloomed in the Hampstead garden and everything came to life. Even Henry was in a better mood. One afternoon, he came in from the shed whistling, carrying a cardboard box with him. He placed it on the chair beside him and sat down at the table.

Carla was itching to ask what the box contained. More Post-its? Paper supplies? More hats and costumes? Perhaps an admiral's hat this time? She imagined her husband dressed as a maritime captain.

"The story is really coming along," he said happily. "Amazing what a little sunshine and brightness can do. I feel completely inspired." He pushed his mug at Carla. "Soon I'll be finished."

She nodded and refilled it.

"Maybe when I'm done, we can take that holiday you wanted. A little break in the Lake District."

"Oh, Henry, that would be fabulous!"

"Well, don't get too excited. I just need to work out a few more things. I'm having problems with the plot, but it's nothing I can't fix. Anyway, time waits for no man. I must get back. I'm in mid discovery and if I don't continue, I'll forget everything before I can put it down on paper."

"But I prepared lunch. I thought I'd set up the things in the garden and we could have a little picnic. Or we could watch a bit of telly and eat off the TV trays. Come on, Henry, loosen up. Live a little."

"I'll eat something later. I'm not hungry, Carla. Plus, who says I'm not enjoying my life now? For years I've been going through the motions, but this is what I'm meant to be doing." Henry's eyes shone, bright and glossy. "I'll be outside in my office if you need me," he said, grabbing a handful of carrot batons and pecking her on the cheek on his way out.

Carla looked over at the food she'd prepared, picked up the dish holding the crudités she'd painstakingly shaped into flowers and leaves so that they resembled a garden. With a steady hand, she hurled it with all her force against the back door.

OCTOBER CAME ALONG and Mother Nature couldn't make up her mind. The morning started off with drizzle and fog; two minutes later the sun came out, then chill would freeze the ground, before it finally settled into a pleasant autumnal afternoon.

Henry startled his wife one afternoon by quietly walking into the house. He was cradling a Tesco shopping bag bulging with papers.

"What are you doing back so soon?" Carla asked.

"It's nearly two o'clock, Carla."

"Is it? Oh, goodness, you must be famished. Do you want me to make you a sandwich and a nice cup of tea?"

He shook his grey head, looking miserable.

"What's wrong, Henry?"

He shook his head again and wiped his nose.

"You aren't getting sick, are you?" she asked alarmed.

"No, no . . . I feel fine. Sit down. Please don't start fussing, Carla."

"What is it, then?"

"I'm just having problems with the story," he said, signalling a manila folder he retrieved from the bag. "I sent out a few chapters to two different literary consultants to get feedback, but they both said the same thing: they don't think my story is good enough."

Carla stared at the folder. At the corner of each sheet of paper was a neatly underlined title that read: *The Shed*. Why on earth would he be writing about their shed? The eye patch and strange hat she'd seen him wearing that day in the garden made her think perhaps he'd been writing about buccaneers or a sea voyage. She was dying to ask a million questions, but his face was dark with silence.

"It takes time, Henry. You'll get there in the end." She squeezed his hand.

"Of course I'll get *there*. I never said I wouldn't get *there*."

"I was just saying maybe you need to think about things in a different way, approach it from a new angle, then maybe you'll be able to solve the structural problems. You have to be willing to experiment with your story. Make sacrifices. You must be prepared to kill off your darlings."

Henry stared at Carla for a few moments without saying a word. "Never mind," he finally said. "Forget I mentioned it. What would you know about writing a story anyway? I'm sure the ending will work itself out in time."

Carla stood in the kitchen staring at her slippers, feeling stupid and useless.

Henry picked up his folder and placed it in the plastic bag. Without another word, he walked back into the rain.

He finished his novel in December. Carla was selecting Christmas cards to put up on the mantel, when Henry ran in breathless.

"It turned out you were right. The ending wasn't working, so I threw away the last forty pages and started over again. This new story is even better," he said.

"That's great, Henry. That's really wonderful."

"I have written three hundred and twenty-seven pages in total, Carla. Can you believe it? Barely a year and over three hundred pages to show for it. Pretty soon I'll be able to send it out. I'm sure this time someone will want to publish it. You know what? We should celebrate. Tonight. Go out somewhere nice. You can get all prettied up. What do you think about that?"

Carla nodded and bit her lip, reaching over to the tree and adjusting a light bulb that had gone out.

"That's a lovely idea, Henry. Just lovely."

LATER, AS THEY sat together at the Hungry Steer, Carla in a light-blue dress that set off her eyes and Henry in a dark suit, he called over the waiter and ordered a bottle of house wine to toast his new novel.

"Cheers to the most talented man in the world!"

Henry clinked her glass and smiled like a new father.

"And now I have a little something to celebrate as well," Carla said, suddenly feeling shy and nervous.

"Oh?" said Henry, starting on his sirloin steak.

"I wanted to save it for a big surprise on Christmas Day, but now is as good a time as any."

"Well spit it out, woman. Out with it."

"Well, only . . . I just thought . . . I wanted to tell you before. Do you remember that writing contest? The one you said was a scam?"

"Oh, spit it out already, Carla. What is it?"

"I wrote a story."

Henry's mouth dropped open and a piece of steak fell out.

"A story?" he repeated, his voice heavy with disbelief.

"Yes."

"Are you sure?"

"Yes. Why is that so surprising? Why can't I be a writer too? I am a creative person, Henry. I have ideas."

"How long were you going to keep this from me?" he said, putting down his cutlery.

"I didn't do it on purpose. I told you, I wanted to surprise you. And before . . . well, it was just that you were so engrossed in your work I didn't think you cared, really. It isn't like I've done anything wrong, Henry. I've been there for you all this time. I'm still here."

"Did you finish it?"

"Beg your pardon?"

"Did you finish your story?"

"Yes," she said, her face a mixture of pride and defiance.

"When?"

"Some months ago."

"I mean, when did you have time?"

"I found time, Henry."

"And did you . . . did you send it off?"

"Yes," she said softly, reaching into her handbag and producing a glossy Christmas issue of *Writer's Magazine*. In a corner was a beaming Carla, holding up a small gold mosquito-shaped trophy. Underneath, in bold, was her name and the words: "1st prize winner".

A horrible expression crossed Henry's face.

"I thought you would be proud of me."

"Shhh!" Henry said, putting his hand out like a crossing guard and cocking his head.

Their table was facing a large well-pruned garden with pine trees and evergreens. Carla followed Henry's eyes and noticed the tops of the trees swaying in the wind. A blue bolt of lightning suddenly illuminated the sky.

Henry stood up. "It's time to go."

"But we haven't even finished our meals."

"Now, Carla! Can't you see it's going to rain? We need to get back."

"Henry, please listen to me," she said in the car. "It was just a silly idea at first. I thought it would be interesting if we both had the same hobby. I wasn't serious about it, not at the beginning, but then I found I enjoyed it and I was good at it. I didn't mean to upset you. I thought you would be happy. There is really nothing to be upset about."

"Be quiet," he said abruptly.

"At first I didn't want to bother you and then . . . I got scared, Henry. I just didn't know how to tell you. Then later when they sent me a letter and said they wanted to publish it . . ."

"Shut up!" he roared, rolling down his window. "Do you hear that?"

At first Carla heard nothing, but then an eerie piercing sound, high pitched like a ghost wail, made her teeth chatter.

"We have to hurry home," said Henry.

It was a race to beat the storm home. But no matter how fast Henry sped, he couldn't outrun it. By the time he pulled up to their driveway, the sky had turned black, and hailstones the size of golf balls were pouring down on their cul-de-sac. Carla sat frozen in the car, watching as the hail turned into sheets of blinding rain, screeching and whistling and threatening to destroy everything in its path.

With a sound that was even scarier than the storm, Henry opened the car door and fell out. "Oh, God, the shed," he cried.

The wind shrieked at Henry like a demented witch.

"Where are the nails?" he screamed.

"The what?"

"*The fucking nails*, Carla. Fetch me a hammer, too. The shed is going to cave in."

"You aren't going to climb up there, are you?"

"Out of my way."

He ran out to the garden and hauled a short ladder to the side of the shed, holding the nails in his mouth.

"Henry, Henry! Get down from there, right now."

"Curse you to hell, woman. I swear I will be gone by morning if you don't go inside and let me be," he bellowed.

Carla watched from the kitchen window as her husband

hammered like a man possessed, nailing pieces of canvas and planks every which way in order to reinforce the roof. At one point, the hammer slipped and came down on his thumb. Even with the back door closed, Carla could make out his enraged curses. But Henry was made of tougher stuff than a mere hammer blow; it was still a race between her husband and the storm, and crouched like an animal on top of the shed, he had no intention of losing. For every corner the wind tore or lifted, Henry immediately hammered in ten steel-headed nails – until he ran out of ammunition. Then, with a desperation on his face she had never seen before, he threw himself bodily on top of the roof. But it was no use. The wind, in one final scream of victory, triumphantly swept off the entire thing: tarp, nails, planks of wood, Henry and all.

The shed lay bare with its frail, naked beams exposed. Carla could see the soup tin minus its sharpened pencils laying on its side, the multi-coloured Post-it notes, the sodden pirate hat and old Corona typewriter. The cardboard box that had formerly contained stacks of neatly typed paper was empty, the pages flitting here and there in the garden.

Henry jumped up and down trying to catch them with his arms outstretched, reminding Carla of a young boy chasing his first butterfly.

"Henry," she called out, wanting to tell him his pages could still be salvaged. Everything was going to be fine and together they would fix what was damaged.

"Henry –"

"Leave me alone!" he shouted, turning and slipping heavily on a wet slab of concrete. The few sodden pages he'd collected fell from his hands. Carla stood rooted to her spot in front of the window, watching as Henry crawled in the grass, sobbing great ragged sobs, his arms reaching up while his stories swirled into a vicious cyclone of white and were carried up into the sky.

THE LANGUAGE OF TREES

MARTHA ALICIA ALZIBAR, twelve years and nine months of age, had been sent to live with her grandparents in Manantial after the unexpected death of her mother Alma.

A stern grey-faced nun walked her to the station, and after placing a hardened roll wrapped in a napkin in one hand and a note for her grandparents in the other, she prayed for the girl's soul, whispering something about not letting the sins of the mother fall upon the child.

As Martha stepped off the train, Grandfather Antonio took in her worn shoes, striped dress and the battered valise she clutched against her body. Martha looked nothing at all like her mother, who had been tall and rosy-cheeked. His granddaughter was small and dark with pinched features, but she had the same determined little chin. Antonio would have recognised that chin anywhere.

Antonio held his hand out. "You must be Martha."

In response the little girl threw her thin arms around his neck.

"How was your trip? Are you hungry?" he asked, trying to unwrap himself from her grasp.

She stared at him with sad, empty eyes. At a loss for what to say, Antonio reached into the pockets of his trousers and produced a handful of caramels.

"Grandmama will not allow me to have these. Can you believe it? A man as old as I am and not able to eat what he wants." Grandfather made a clicking sound with his tongue. "Will you help me get rid of them? Because if you don't and she catches me, I'll be in hot soup. *Aye*, speaking of soup, Grandmama will be upset if I don't get you home for the evening meal. She's making a spring-chicken-and-vegetable soup," he said, rubbing his hands together like a cricket. "You like chicken?"

The girl continued to regard him silently, her small dry lips opening and closing like the mouth of a goldfish.

Antonio wondered if she even knew how to speak at all. Sister Elena never said anything about a deaf-mute girl. Putting the sweets back into his pocket, Grandfather led the way outside.

"This is my pride and joy," he said, stopping at a rusty vehicle parked some distance from the station. "Isn't he a beauty? I call him Pedro." Grandfather pounded the side of the door with the palm of his hand until it opened. "Do you know why I call him Pedro?" he asked as he helped Martha into the truck. "My donkey was named Pedro. And now this is my favourite pain in the ass." He guffawed, slapping the top of his thigh. "You don't find my jokes funny, eh? Well, neither does your grandmother."

They drove together without saying much for some miles. Now and then, Antonio would point out a landmark or make a silly remark, but the little girl remained silent. It wasn't until the main road turned into the narrow dirt lane that led to the village, that Martha showed any signs of life. Then she sat straight up in the passenger seat and watched with amazement as the landscape unfolded like something out of a picture book.

The day was a perfect one. Manantial's crystal lakes reflected the trees that stood at attention like giant sentinels dotting the countryside. They were so tall their branches seemed to touch the sky, which in itself was a marvel: an impossible, unreal blue, like a book of watercolour paintings she had once seen.

A tiny picturesque village, ninety kilometres from any notable town, Manantial was renowned for its lakes, verdant forests and its stubborn reluctance to embrace modern industry. Most of its population of 754 residents were distantly related in some way or another, with everyone knowing everyone's business and hardly a secret between them. Church, gossip and disagreements were the universally approved activities; strangers, alcohol and television considered suspect.

"Welcome to your new home," said Antonio, gesturing at the landscape as if he himself were responsible. "Breathtaking, isn't it? This land is a very special, unique place."

"Grandpapa," said Martha in a whisper, "my mama told me about it. It is exactly the way I imagined it from her stories."

Antonio was so shocked to hear his granddaughter speak that he almost ran Pedro into a nearby ditch.

"Alma told stories?"

"Oh, yes. Mama told wonderful ones. Sometimes I would ask her to make them up for me, but other times she told me ones she'd heard when she was a little girl. She always said you were her favourite storyteller in the whole world, Grandpapa."

Antonio felt a familiar, painful lump at the back of his throat.

When Alma was a child she had been his light – inquisitive, bright and loving – the only certainty that his miserable existence had been for something. Beautiful as well as obedient, Alma was helpful with chores, charitable, studious and sweet.

Everyone who met her loved her; such was her charm and grace. But upon reaching her fifteenth birthday, his daughter began to turn wild. Trouble soon followed, and when she started slipping out at night to meet with the butcher's boy, his wife, Inez, packed her off to the Sisters of Mercy, a convent in the remote mountains of San Sebastian. No one thought the punishment too severe, as the village had its share of sons and daughters who were sent to study and work in the bigger towns and cities. Alma, however, never spoke to her parents again. They didn't even know they had a grandchild, had never seen a photograph, until the sisters at the hospital wrote to inform them of their daughter's death.

Antonio and Inez had waited such a long time to have a baby, but the doctors said there was little they could do and any child would be a miracle. When Alma finally arrived, she was such a beautiful, joyous baby it seemed God had blessed them for their patience. Later, when she started sneaking around with boys and lying, Antonio felt betrayed. His daughter had become a frivolous young woman and he wondered if having her had been a mistake. When Inez sent her away, his sense of pride didn't allow him to intervene. He always assumed that one day Alma would repent of her actions and return home.

With the recent news of her death something inside him broke and disappeared into the earth along with her body. Now, sitting here beside him was the only thing that connected him to his beloved daughter.

Antonio stopped to wipe his face with the back of his calloused hand.

"A long, long time ago," he said, "part of the land you see before you was one of the three paradises, which the Gods created for their own pleasure. The Penchua forest ran the length from where the sun rises to where the sun sets, near the lake that looks like a mirror. Many wide rivers and lakes criss-crossed the area, some meeting at the top, some on the bottom, and in that manner they watered the entire country

– that is why everything was so green and lush.

"The Gods named it *Manantial* – which means stemming from water.

"When the Spanish came with their special rulers to mark off the land, they had their own name for it. They called it the Emerald Forest.

"Strange and vibrantly coloured animals lived within the canopy of the giant trees, some of which soared thousands of feet into the air. These trees were said to be average size compared to the Gods, who created them in their own image. The more revered ones grew under odd and special circumstances, such as the Regulu, whose bark and trunk are never exposed to sunlight, and which grows only at night by the glow of the moon; or the Ligonessa, which is said to house a special lemony-coloured bird that could mimic every single sound."

"Every sound?" said the amazed girl.

"Like this one," and Grandfather did one of his special birdcalls for Martha.

"After many years, the Gods grew lonely and decided to share their wonderful paradise. The simple condition was that their guests, the humans, had to respect nature in all its forms.

"So the people applied themselves to learning about every tree, every branch and every fruit, including all the curative properties. For example, did you know that, delicately extracted, the leaves of the Ligonessa can heal almost anything? Did you also know that the Voldrevi plant has tiny berries which, if picked at the right time of year and crushed into a root tea of bitter herbs, could prolong your life?" Grandfather chuckled.

"The people studied all these things and more. They used the cures, but they always thought first to ask permission of the trees and plants, because that was the way things were back then; people had respect.

"The older, wiser humans became special envoys – 'shaman' they were called. They understood nature in all her manifestations and could communicate with the Gods, speaking the language of the trees.

"Each shaman had a spiritual companion tree, considered to be ancient bearers of knowledge. They were taught the secrets of shape shifting. In the flash of an eye a shaman could transform into a lynx, a jaguar, or even take on the form of another human. Above all this enabled them to help the people understand each other. And for a time everyone lived in peaceful harmony, without any wars . . ."

He glanced at his granddaughter who was so entranced she hadn't noticed they'd arrived at the gate.

"We're here, Martha," he said smiling.

"Grandpapa, why is it forbidden to have any sweets? Is Grandmama very strict?"

Antonio was silent for a few moments. "Well, it is forbidden for me. I'm diabetic, you see. It means I can't have anything good to eat."

She gazed at him with unfathomable eyes. "No caramels?"

"No."

"No soda pop?"

"No."

"No cake or pie?"

"I'm afraid not. No sweets, no sugar, nothing too salty or too spicy. She makes me drink my coffee black," he said, shaking his head as if his body were playing a great joke on him, depriving him of all the good things in life.

Before they reached the door, Antonio dipped into his pocket and pulled out a handful of caramels. Smiling, he put a conspiratorial finger to his lips, showing his toothless grin.

And the little girl, who hadn't eaten since her mother's funeral, gobbled them.

"MARTHA! FINISH YOUR breakfast so I can brush your hair," said Grandmama, wiping her hands on her starched apron and coming over to inspect the girl's braids. Uncoiled, the freed tresses flowed down her back and past her waist, threatening to spill on to the clean kitchen floor.

"Ay, but this will not do!" Inez said as she took a thin steel comb and began the process of taming. She yanked the comb from the roots down through Martha's unruly curls pulling through the knots until the locks were smooth and tangle free. Then she started at the top again – pull, drag, down, up; pull, drag, down, up – keeping rhythm with the meter of her favourite discourse – a rant on the manners and discipline of children nowadays, blaming the failures of the world on their selfish ways and the lack of respect afforded parents.

"Not so tight, Inez," said Grandfather, seeing Martha wince.

"Bah," she said, shooting her husband a dirty look. "And what would you know about hair? You don't even have any hair, old man."

With every verbal emphasis, for every perceived slight, she dug deeper and deeper into the scalp, until Martha wanted to scream.

Grandmama didn't stop until the result was a set of perfectly matched and shiny braids.

"There," she said, admiring her handiwork. "Now your hair is set in the way most becoming a proper young lady. Now off with you to school." And with that, she turned briskly to her plucked chickens.

Antonio eyed his grandchild sitting across the table, unhappily trying to hide the tears the problematic hair had caused. It wasn't that Inez wasn't fond of Martha; Grandmama was just disciplined, that was all. She approved of order and a fastidious neatness that had taken a lifetime to perfect. Sometimes, God bless, the granddaughter could be trying. Grandfather slid his coffee cup to her and put his fingers to his lips.

FEBRUARY 1963 WENT on record as being the hottest month the citizens of Manantial had ever known. The two-mile walk to school took Martha twice as long as it normally would, partially because she was unaccustomed to the long country roads, but mainly because of the heat. Four weeks of scorching relentlessness and thirty-five-degree days had turned the lush crops a toasted-almond colour, causing the cows to halt production and the local children to go without their morning milk.

The heatwave, not seen in that part of the world for hundreds of years, sparked a tremendous debate among the villagers. Everything from issues of religion and faith – was God punishing them for unconfessed sins? – to the best way to combat the drought. Saint Teresa, or "Teresita", as the denizens dubbed her, patron saint of bountiful harvest, overnight became a celebrity, a dozen makeshift altars popping up throughout the countryside in her honour.

There was also some contention about when the heatwave began.

Some villagers claimed it started precisely at 2:49 p.m. on January 11, during the Sweetheart Coronation, when Carnival Princess Mayte Fernandez – sporting a fur cape, a four-inch beehive and the look of a determined martyr – fainted from a combination of heat exhaustion and paint fumes from her not-yet-dry gilded throne. Others insisted it had started four days before, around the time Martha Alicia Alzibar came to live in Manantial.

When she'd first started at Bolivar Elementary School, the

children had looked Martha over, pronounced her weird and, aside from the occasional teasing, had ignored her. But that was just as well because the kids at school would never learn her secret.

Martha was going to make it rain.

She had it all planned out. She would be renowned for being the girl who stopped the drought. The villagers would bear her on their shoulders and hold a special three-day festival in her honour. Grandmama would be so proud she would forget her rancour and hug Martha. The children would beg for her to tell them how she made it rain. If they were nice, she might even oblige.

Martha had read in a book that people with special powers and large amounts of faith could do anything they put their minds to; they could even move mountains. The nuns at the hospital had said that if she prayed hard enough, her mama would make a recovery. But as much as she tried, it hadn't worked. Maybe it was her inexperience, but the nuns said it was because she had no faith. One needed shut-eyed communion to speak to God. The sisters looked at the sad-faced girl with the ragamuffin dress and squirrel-tail hair, and shook their heads. On the registration form, under Faith, Alma had scrawled "none".

"If God is not with you, how can you expect others to be?" they wondered.

At lunchtime, the children were found drooped and wilted in small colourful clusters scattered around the school grounds like wild flowers. Martha lay on the warm grass and finding it too hot to eat or read, concentrated instead on using her energy to will a patch of rain over the school.

Martha closed her eyes in order to outline the perfect nimbus in her mind. Concentration: all the books said whatever you wanted to happen you needed concentration. After a few minutes of visualisation, she began to meditate – then the problem of the chanting began. Would it be considered chanting if she recited it inwardly or did chanting only work out loud? She debated for a while, before compromising by mumbling softly.

She remained that way almost the entire lunch period, and was just thinking about giving up when she felt a small drop on her cheek. Her heart began to beat wildly as she struggled to slow her breathing. It couldn't be. The chanting had worked?

Wait . . . There! There it was again, another small drop, this time in the region of her chin. She was certain it had worked now – the book had been right.

Martha had made it rain.

Slowly, she sat up, opening first one eye, then the other, to find herself face to face not with a black cumulus, not even a grey one. Instead, she encountered three pairs of laughing brown eyes. She sat up quickly to the teasing laughter of her classmates.

"Hey, Martha, were you praying or casting spells?"

Wiping the spittle from her face, she thumbed in the direction of the sweaty boys, demanding, "Who do you think you are, slobbering on me like that?"

"He's Pablo, he is Andres, and I am Roberto," indicated a tall boy. "And my mama says you are a freak and a witch!"

She felt her face burn.

It was true that a few of the more superstitious villagers believed the heatwave coincided with the girl's arrival. It was also true that Martha didn't have the comportment of a country child. She was paler and skinnier than her peers and was often seen having conversations with herself as she walked to and from school. And the animals: who could explain the animals? Martha would often be found taking nibbles and scraps she kept in a basket to stray horses, pigs and chickens, petting and christening them with elaborate, double-barrelled names. The local children were taught from infancy their proper place over all God's beasts and creatures. Animals were for eating and working the fields, not for cuddling.

Then there were the books. Martha was always engrossed in books and drawings, using a small slate upon which she noted cryptic marks and characters. "Why can't she play like a normal child?" they asked one another – not imagining that words could ever compete against a clear blue sky or a healthy yellow sun.

But what really bothered the villagers – more than the animals and the books – was the simple matter of heathenism. As far as they knew, the girl had never been baptised. Although no one had the nerve to mention it to her grandparents.

Roberto picked up Martha's book bag with his foot and flung it towards Andres. "Let's see what the little witch has inside."

The boys erupted into wild laughter again.

"Throw it to me, throw it to me," shouted Pablo. "I want to see."

"You are such ignorant donkeys," said Martha, scrambling to her feet.

"Look, if it isn't a spell book," said Andres, pulling out a handsome red leather book with embossed golden lettering. He threw it to Pablo who caught it with one hand. Pablo flung it over his head at Roberto, who caught it under his leg.

"This must be the secret of all her power."

"Quick, check inside and see if there is a spell to make it rain."

"Let's play keep away," said Pablo.

"No! Give it back to me right now, you jerk."

"Oh-oh, Pablo! You better hope she doesn't place a spell on you."

Then Roberto had the idea of tearing out the pages and launching them into the air like airplanes.

"Look, they fly really well," he said.

"Let me see that. *Mira.* I can do better."

"No!' she cried out. "No!"

Martha bit her bottom lip so they wouldn't see her cry. The book was special: magical, irreplaceable. It had been given to her on her twelfth birthday and on the back cover it was inscribed in Alma's florid handwriting: *To my beloved daughter . . .*

The boys were so entertained by the paper airplanes that they didn't notice Martha retrieve her bag or when she approached Roberto and placed a sharpened pencil near his head.

"You know what will happen if I ram this into your ear, you little shit?" she said in a very quiet voice. "You will be drooling like an idiot boy and pissing in your pants for the rest of your life. You think I'm a witch, right? See what happens if you don't. Now give me back my book and pick up all those pages you tore off."

Roberto did as he was told but the other two boys ran off to fetch the teacher.

They found the strange girl sitting on the grass, cradling her damaged pages against her chest and reciting an old English nursery rhyme. The children, not understanding the words, later told their parents that Martha Alzibar had been uttering curses.

WHEN MARTHA CAME home that day, Grandmother Inez was waiting for her. "I have never been so embarrassed in all my life," she said, slamming her paring knife down on to the counter. "And from whom do I hear the news while I'm at the market today? That terrible gossip Estella, that's who. She tells me with tears in her eyes that you tried to attack Pablito. How do you think I feel, Martha? I see these women in church every week and now I can't even look them in the eye."

"Well, she's lying because it wasn't Pablo, Grandmama. It was Roberto and I was going to –"

"SILENCIO!" roared Inez, turning towards her granddaughter. "How could you threaten to hurt those boys for a simple game? They were only playing."

"They had my book," said Martha.

"A book? A stupid book and you were going to maim Roberto? Did the devil get into you, girl? I don't know what you think we do around these parts, but I won't condone this behaviour. I want you to go to your room right now." And with that Inez grabbed Martha by her hair, twisting and twisting until it felt as if the braids were going to rip off in her hands.

When Antonio came in from work, he found his wife sitting at the table, staring at the pieces of potato scattered all over the floor.

"Inez, what's going on? Did something happen to Martha?"

"'What happened to Martha? What happened to Martha?'" she mimicked. "Ask your precious granddaughter, why don't you? She's turning out to be more and more like her mother every day. I guess it's true what they say about the sins of the father . . ."

"That girl needs us, Inez. Rather than helping her, you choose to be judgemental?"

"Only the good Lord above is fit to judge. And who knows why he decided to curse me not only with that raggedy bastard, but also with her whoring mother." Grandmama looked heavenward and made a rapid sign of the cross.

"Oh, Inez," said Antonio sadly, "sometimes I don't understand you."

Ignoring him, his wife stood to her full height. "What's done is done. But I tell you, if she doesn't shape up, she will go the same way as her mother." Then, as if noticing the floor for the first time, she exclaimed, "Would you look at what that child has made me do? Look at this mess! Who is going to clean it up?" She picked up the broom and began to sweep potatoes in the direction of her husband.

"Listen, Inez," he said, firmly grabbing her arm. "If you drive her away . . . If you drive Martha away, the way you did Alma, you will have to deal with me. Do you understand?"

"Don't be stupid, Antonio," hissed Grandmother.

Inez and Alma had always had a strained relationship. Although Martha's mother was an obedient child who did all of her chores and was helpful to her parents without being asked, Inez still found much to fault. She was only trying to help, of course, but Alma took her suggestions the wrong way and learned to be restrained and cautious around her mother. With Antonio, on the other hand, Alma was loving and tender. Inez tried to pretend it didn't bother her that the two of them had a special bond and were always laughing and playing their private games and jokes. One of their favourites was one in which they pretended Inez was invisible and couldn't hear or see as they whispered and gestured behind her back.

Lately, Grandmama had noticed he did the same thing with Martha.

Except for the uncontrollable hair, the granddaughter really didn't resemble her mother at all. Alma at her age had been full of life, but Martha had the look of an older person instead of a child. She had a strange disquieting air that Inez couldn't put her finger on, as if she was hiding something or had a secret she couldn't wait to tell.

Once, Martha confided that her mama came to visit her in her dreams.

"Does she say anything?" demanded Inez.

"Of *course*. She talks to me all the time."

"Well, what does she say, child? Out with it."

"Oh, this and that. She tells me to be good and obey you and Grandfather. She also said to tell you not to pull my hair."

Inez shivered in her bones when she heard this. But a talking ghost was an impossibility. Everyone knows the dead can't speak.

"She doesn't mean it you know. She can't help the things she says," said Grandfather, as he tucked Martha into bed. "She has a fierce temper, but she cares for you. I know she does."

"She said I was a very wicked girl, Grandpapa," she said, wiping her eyes. "But it wasn't my fault. Those boys took the book my mama gave me."

Grandfather gingerly took the ragged tome from under her pillow and placed it and all its torn pages on the nightstand.

"A pencil was too good for that Roberto if you ask me. Next time they bother you let me know and I will give you my fishing knife."

He tried to catch her eye, to let her know he understood, but she wouldn't look at him. He tucked the sheet around her bed. "Do you want to hear a story?"

Martha turned to stare at the wall.

"Very well then," said Grandfather, clearing his throat, "I will tell you a story of the Red Ribbons.

"Many moons ago, before my great-great-grandfather was born, the people of Manantial used to have festivals to celebrate the trees. These festivals were held during the summer and winter seasons and everyone partook of drink and special dishes like the ones we have during carnival. The branches of the trees were adorned with special ribbons. Red, like the ones you wear in your hair, Martha. The young village maidens wore crowns of flowers and leaves in their hair, and translucent gowns like the wings of a butterfly, so beautiful that the silk worms were jealous. Sometimes in their happiness and joy, the maidens would dance around naked under the trees. But no one laughed or frowned, because they were worshipping nature.

"The girls wore no gold or silver on their necks or arms, as metals were not allowed near the trees, but their hands and faces were decorated with special dye made from plants – ochre and reds, deep like sweet berry juice.

"Every year the three prettiest girls were selected to be the carnival sweethearts and the shaman drew circles and planets and shell symbols on the backs of their hands and necks, so that everyone would know how special they were.

"The tradition has continued to this day, Martha. We start the celebrations tomorrow. You will love it, child. Three days of feasts and all the wonderful foods, drink and treats you can eat. Everyone dresses up and there are plays, poems and games. Your mother Alma was carnival princess, you know, and your grandmother before that."

"Grandmama?" said the girl in amazement.

"Inez, in her youth, was the most beautiful girl I ever laid eyes on. She had long dark hair and a wonderful smile. She wore her hair in braids with red ribbons, just like you," he said, kissing Martha on her forehead. "Now go to sleep and stop worrying about your book. We can take it to be repaired in town. What do you think about that? I'm sure the leathermaker can fix the stitching and make it good as new." He patted her on the shoulder. "Sleep well, my child."

BUT THAT NIGHT Martha had a terrible dream. A group of young girls were dancing in white flowing gowns beneath the moonlight. Instead of braids, their wavy hair blew loose and wild in the wind. A young man watched from the shadows as they danced. He held a sharp knife in one hand and in the other a length of red ribbon. The girls were too busy frolicking to notice him approaching, until it was too late. As the man yanked the closest one back by her scalp, the maiden turned to scream. In the dream she had looked just like her mother.

THE NEXT DAY at breakfast, Martha's eyes were red and swollen.

"I don't know what you were thinking, Antonio, filling her head with useless stories. Can't you see the state of the child? She obviously hasn't had a decent night's sleep. Ay, but just look at that hair."

Grandmama unpinned the braids and brushed out the thick hair in silence. Then, hands on her hips, she looked critically at Martha.

"I think you should wear it down today. It is a special day, after all."

She took one of the red ribbons from the table and smoothing it out with her hand, wrapped it under Martha's hair and tied it on top in a bow.

"Now hurry or you will be late. And don't forget to come straight home from school so you can do your chores in time for the festival."

THE SCHOOL DAY seemed unbearably long. Martha couldn't wait for the lessons to be over. The children were too excited about the upcoming festival to bother with teasing, but Pablo and Andres amused themselves by throwing pieces of chalk in her direction when the teacher wasn't looking.

""Hey, Martha, where are your braids today?"

"*Mira*, doesn't she look more and more like a witch every day?"

"Oops, better be careful, she's getting her pencil out."

Without a word, Roberto turned away from his friends, concentrating on the board. Andres and Pablo exchanged glances, but soon they followed suit and left Martha alone.

It wasn't the first time Martha had been teased by the boys. On her third day of school, they had followed her home. They threw pebbles at her legs, snorted and made loud piggy noises. "Martha loves dirty animals. Martha is ugly like a dog with mange. Martha has no mother or father."

WHEN THE BELL marked the end of the last lesson, the children rushed home to have their baths. Martha, relieved to escape the sweltering heat of the classroom, filed out with them, but instead of going straight home as instructed, she went to the library.

This was her favourite place in the world. The quiet, sunny room didn't have many books, but the smell of the old musty volumes reminded her of the times she spent with her mother visiting the municipal library in San Sebastian.

Olga, the custodian, acknowledged Martha with a curt nod. "We close early today, so hurry."

"Oh," said Martha, disappointed. "I wanted to get a special book today. I don't have to go back to school till Tuesday."

"Tonight is the start of the festival. Why bother with reading when there are so many other things to do?"

Martha didn't have an answer for this. Instead, she went down a dark aisle and played a little game. She chose her book by spinning around three times and pointing randomly wherever her finger landed. After selecting a dictionary, an encyclopedia and a boring book about foot maladies, she decided to try a different approach. She closed her eyes, thinking of a number and stopping at the required amount of steps.

26, 27, 28, 29 ... And that is how she happened upon a little glass shelf at the back of the library that she'd never seen. At the top, sitting all alone, was a red leather book very similar to the one her mother had given her. Reaching up and taking it from the shelf, she brushed off the dust and sat on the floor using her schoolbag as a cushion.

"*Oyé*, little girl. Hurry it up. I have an appointment with the salon and I'm going to be late," called out the librarian.

"Just a few more minutes, Señora Olga."

The book was old. So old its thin onion pages felt like they would dissolve under her fingers. While hers was a fairy-tale book, this one looked as if it had been made for grown-ups. Sometimes it was handwritten in a long scrolling script and other times it was printed with unusual serifs. Sometimes it was only blank pages accompanied by drawings. A few of the pictures were gruesome and detailed. People lying on altars with their heads chopped off and girls dancing around a large pointed totem. Others she didn't understand, even when she held the book upside down. At the back there was a fancy colour illustration of a man who looked remarkably like her grandfather.

Martha peered at the picture in disbelief. He had the same hair, beard and kindly wise eyes. But instead of the plaid shirt and trousers that Grandfather wore, he had a loincloth and beads around his neck. A brilliant crown of blood-red feathers sat on his head, the points bending in the wind as if he were wearing streamers. Under the image was a caption. *Timota: Wise Shamanic Ruler of Manantial, Interpreter of the Language of Trees, 1629.*

Martha scrambled to her feet.

"Señora Olga? . . . Señora Olga?" she called out. "I'm finished. I have to go home now. Hello? Is anyone there? Señora Olga?"

The front desk was empty. Martha took out a pencil and wrote the librarian a note letting her know she was borrowing the book.

Outside, she shielded her eyes against the brilliant sun. The schoolyard was completely deserted, the ground so white and scorching she could feel the heat through her shoes and socks. If she took a short cut through the forest, not only would it be cooler, but if she hurried, she might make it in time to do her chores. Normally Martha would have stayed on the country roads as she'd been advised, but as Grandmama said, today was a special day.

The afternoon was silent as the girl made her way from the schoolyard to the woods. She stopped several times to observe the lack of tweet or croak. Even the birds and frogs must be preparing for tonight. The trees rustled and shook their parched leaves as if agreeing with Martha.

Grateful to be out of the sun, she decided to take off her shoes. The pleasant touch of cool, soft moss reminded her of carpeting.

This is what it must feel like to be a wood nymph, she thought, spinning around and around with her arms stretched out, so that her hair fanned out like she was underwater.

She was reminded of one of the images she'd seen in the old book at the library.

Reaching into her bag, she took the book out and sat on a nearby stump to read the first story.

Once upon a time a young warrior named Atoucan saw a girl wearing a garland of flowers and dancing around a fire. He was immediately enchanted and plotted to steal her away. And so it was that during the night Atoucan stole Saruxa under his arm, the way one would take a bundle of firewood or a suckling pig. The girl screamed, demanding to be put down, but Atoucan was maddened with the moonlight and his desire and would not be stopped.

When Timota, the great Shaman, discovered that Saruxa had been abducted, he fell into a fury. He conspired with the trees to learn the whereabouts of the couple.

Saruxa was found drowned in Lake Manacu the following day.

Timota's rage didn't stop there.

The next day two maidens disappeared while they were in the forest gathering berries. The third day, another one vanished into thin air. No one could understand how it happened, but some said they were lifted by the tree branches and taken deep into the ground, never to be seen again. All that was left were their hair ribbons.

Armed with torches, the villagers, led by Atoucan, stormed the woods and found the hiding place of the Shaman.

"You can't hurt me," he said. "I am the emissary to the forest and only I can speak to the trees. What will you do without my help?"

They strung him up by his feet and slit his throat from ear to ear, so he never again had a reason to speak.

Then they burned the trees.

They say the sound of the screaming trees was like the high-pitched sound of a woman or a wounded animal.

The land responded with a terrible drought. For eighteen months, nothing grew in Manantial. The treeless plains grew parched and dry and yielded no crops or food.

The people, starving and desperate, wanted to negotiate a truce. But they had forgotten how to speak to the Gods and no one remembered the language of the trees.

"MARTHA, MARTHA."

She stopped reading, listening to a faint faraway noise that sounded like laughter.

Pushing back her hair from her sweaty forehead, she put the book back in her schoolbag and started walking quickly through the forest. When she heard the sound a second time, she turned her head in the direction of the noise to see a patch of darkness dash across the forest.

"Who is it? Is that you, Roberto?"

More faint laughter and the rustling of leaves.

What were those stupid boys up to now? Never mind, she was determined to show them she wasn't frightened.

"Martha, Martha," called a soft voice.

"I'm not scared of you," she called out. She was just as tough as they were; tougher even. Straightening her back and picking up her pace, she decided to ignore them.

After a while the boys must have gotten bored, because there was nothing but silence. She had walked for nearly an hour and through the trees she could see that the sun would soon be setting. Up ahead, she noticed a white object. One of Teresita's altars was erected on a small mound five hundred yards away. Curious, she cut off a branch from a nearby tree to use as a walking stick and climbed up for a closer look. The offering was several stale pieces of bread on a wooden plate, a glass of water, a strand of garlic and the white feathers of a dove. In addition, there was a small box encrusted with bits of glass and tiles. The pattern was delicate, forming a sun that stretched across the top and sides.

Looking to make sure no one was around she carefully picked up the box to study it more closely.

It's Manantial! thought the girl, delighted. Look, there on the back was the crystal lake, with little bits of black glass and milky opals filling in for seagulls and birds. Here were six golden rays dipping into delicate blues and greens, the tiny leaves like a kaleidoscope of apple-pear-green patterns and turquoise and indigo skies.

It was the most beautiful thing Martha had ever seen.

She flipped open the lid to see what wonderful treasure might be contained inside.

What she found made her scream and immediately drop the box. Inside was a long red ribbon attached to . . . No, it couldn't be. Were those bits of hair and something white soaked in blood?

She dropped the box and broke into a run, but didn't get far before she tripped over a root and lost her footing. Down the hill she rolled until she landed on a thick patch of dead leaves and vegetation, hitting her head against a tree.

Martha closed her dazed eyes. As usual she dreamed in stories.

She sat up in alarm. Where was she? How long had she been sleeping? The temperature had begun to cool and long shadows were starting to form on the ground. Martha scrambled to her feet. Her head felt tender and bruised like a melon. She picked dirt out of her skirt and started back towards Teresita's altar.

But the hill seemed enormous and never-ending like a mountain. Martha looked around at the unfamiliar surroundings and realised with a sinking heart that she was lost. It was almost completely dark by now, her head hurt and she was tired.

For the first time she started to feel afraid.

She walked into another clearing, different from the one before. The trees were not like the ones she remembered earlier. These were tall like buildings with trunks as big as houses.

Martha heard a noise behind her – a sound like someone breathing. Spinning around, she tried to identify where it had come from – but heard only the crisp sound of a broken tree branch. She continued to walk and then heard the noise again.

She froze.

"Who's there?" she asked out loud.

Silence.

Quickly, without thinking, she sent out a message to the trees, asking them to be kind to her, to show her the way home. I mean you no harm.

Silence.

Then she heard footsteps.

"Is anyone there?" she whispered.

The branches began to shake and the previously indifferent forest suddenly took on a malevolent air. Martha strangled a wild cry in her throat. Confused, she stumbled, scratching her legs on sharp bramble.

The voices continued. Sometimes they sounded cheerful like children, other times chirpy like birds. Once she thought she heard the sound of her mother crying.

Twice more Martha tripped and picked herself up, the first time tangling her hair on a branch, the second time hitting a tree head on and almost blinding herself.

Whimpering, she limped through the forest as the voices came nearer and nearer, the oppressive evening closing in around her.

Martha, Martha, we want your ribbons red.

Martha, Martha, we want your little head.

MARTHA ALICIA ALZIBAR's body was found floating in Lake Manantial. A brief investigation ensued. Detective Barillo was sent from the capital, but he spent only a few days in Manantial before declaring Martha's death an accident. The consensus among the villagers was that the girl had probably fallen into the lake in the dark and drowned. Grandfather, who had been out that evening searching for her, found nothing but a red ribbon hanging from a tree. Grief-stricken and in shock, Antonio aged ten years overnight. In the throes of a premature stroke, he lost the power of speech and would die a few months after Martha's death.

The residents of Manantial made Barillo nervous with their superstitious nonsense and their distrust of all outsiders. Nonetheless, he called at the church and school and made his enquiries.

Martha's teacher told the inspector that the girl was

obviously troubled; she displayed erratic behaviour and had tried to stab her after recess one day with a pair of scissors. The teacher burst into tears and the baffled detective gallantly lent her his handkerchief.

Several of the children told him that a few days after Martha's disappearance they had seen a small girl in red ribbons walking beside the lane. But the inspector had to scratch that idea as no one could agree on what time they had seen her, just that she appeared to be chanting and walking towards the woods.

A group of farmers mentioned that the girl had brought them bad luck. "She was trouble from the moment we saw her," they said, "just like her mother. Now she's gone and drowned herself in the river." They spat on the soil so her bad luck wouldn't taint them.

Pablo's mother told the inspector that on the night Martha went missing, her son had a dream that he was visited by a tall woman with dark hair, carrying a book. She bent down to kiss him on the forehead and as she did, her face turned into a skeleton.

The inspector wrote down all these little observations in his notepad, but after a few days of half-hearted poking around, he boarded the first train he could to get away from that awful place.

In keeping with the character of Manantial, however, it wasn't what people said that counted; it was what they didn't say.

Inez, for example, never mentioned that on the day Martha went missing she saw her husband leave early and return with mud on his boots.

Esmeralda, who had looked after the church for twenty-two years, did not say she found a dark-red ribbon neatly laid out on the white cloth of the communion altar.

Olga didn't say that the book Martha borrowed had made

its way back into her library.

Grandfather Antonio didn't mention that, on the very afternoon Martha went missing, Grandmama was preparing a chicken and had been so distracted by something at the window she had let the knife slip, cleanly slicing the top of her finger.

And certainly no one ever mentioned that the day after the girl's disappearance, a very large cloud burst over the small village, raining down upon Manantial as if the Gods themselves were weeping.

Two Percent

"You know we're two per cent, right?" says my niece Tatiana when she comes to visit me for the summer.

"What?"

"*Two per cent*," she repeats slowly, as if talking about low-fat milk. "We're two per cent *black*, Auntie Gina." She snaps her gum at me.

Tatiana is my sister's daughter. Just turned sixteen and she's already a stunner: tall and slim, with long legs and an exquisite complexion – a beauty, when not sneering and rolling her eyes.

She has been sent to me by her distraught mother in an attempt to distance her from the unwanted attention of lazy hoodlum boys who have started hanging out near the McDonald's where Tatiana works twice a week.

The boys ride sardine-like, six or seven to a car, my sister tells me. They circle the parking lot waiting for her to emerge, scoffing French fries and milkshakes; like hungry wolves stalking their prey. When she finally exits, they trail her slowly, bestowing compliments like soft kisses. They offer rides, beg for her number; ask if she needs a boyfriend. When all of that fails, they hurl insults.

"Girl, you isn't nuthin' but a skank tease."

Ghetto rats, my sister calls them, even though the term is somewhat inaccurate, living as they do in an affluent suburb.

"At least Tati tells you what's going on," I said to Chloë.

"I don't care about that. She's too young to be chased by boys."

"Relax, sis. She obviously trusts you. You have to trust her back."

"Easy for you to say. You don't have children of your own, Gina. There's a lot of peer pressure. It isn't like when we were kids."

She doesn't mean it the way it comes out, but the words carry a silent accusation. I don't feel the need to remind her that she was just a child herself when she had Tati.

Once upon a time, my sister and I were close, but being a single mother has made Chloë harsh and judgemental; she has no time for anyone who hasn't been in her shoes.

"Later, we're going shopping and then to a movie."

"Not one with too much sex and nudity, I hope?"

"Yeah, right, sis, I'm taking your daughter to a porno. I may not have kids, but that doesn't make me an irresponsible adult, you know."

"Sure, sure. Look, tell her I'll call her in the morning."

AFTER THE MOVIE, Tatiana and I sit in my kitchen slicing tomatoes for our midnight snack.

"So, you interested in anyone at school?" I ask her.

"I dunno," she shrugs, hopping on to the counter. "There's this one guy. He's all right, I guess. But we're just *friends*."

"I had a lot of friends at your age."

"Yeah, my mom told me. But he's an *actual* friend, Auntie Gina." She bites into her sandwich. "I don't even think he knows I like him. Plus, he's got a girl already."

I run a thousand things through my head, wondering what advice, what suggestions I can offer. Not bullshit affirmation-in-the mirror kinds of things, but true learned nuggets, cultivated from years of painful and embarrassing first-hand experiences.

Instead I tell her a story. I tell her how, when she was born, I found Chloë in her hospital gown, crying in front of the baby bassinet.

"'Oh my God, what's wrong?' I asked, scared something had happened to you.

"'Tell me the truth, Gina. Does the baby have all her fingers and toes? The nurses put these little gloves and bootees on her. I think they're hiding something.'

"I wanted to laugh or tease her, tell her you had an extra thumb or something, but your mother looked so worried. I took off the gloves and together we counted your fingers and toes. It took a long time to calm her down."

"I guess Mom was fussing about me even then," says Tati laughing.

"Yeah," I say, "but she's done a great job raising you."

She gives me a lopsided smile and for a moment she looks exactly like my sister did at her age.

DESPITE LIVING IN the shadow of her mother's paranoia, Tatiana is refreshingly laid back. She attends a city school – a subject of much friction between mother and daughter. She likes the people there, she tells me. They're for real, not *fakes*. She doesn't want to transfer to the school her mom is pushing.

"I bet they don't even have any Latinos there."

Tatiana, whose father is of German descent and whose surname is Müeller, has never visited a Spanish-speaking country, doesn't understand a word of the language and has never before expressed interest in her Latin American heritage.

She's about as Latino as that ad for tortilla chips featuring a pretty señorita in a flamenco dress, shaking her hips to salsa music, whilst her partner, in a mariachi hat and Cuban accordion sleeves, attempts to disembowel her with his knee. As the advert pans out, the happy couple dances off into the sunset doing a complicated made-for-television version of the lambada. "Hot, hot, hot," screams the jingle. Spicy corn tortilla chips apparently synonymous with fiery writhing passion and tanned taut Latinos.

"Not to mention I'm two per cent," adds Tatiana.

"What's with all this percentage business anyway? You're not a recipe for margaritas, Tati. A person is more than a sum of all her parts," I say in my wise, grown-up voice.

"See, at school they're always going on about DNA and molecules and stuff. You may not think it, but we all break down into something, Auntie Gina. Into tiny parts no one ever sees."

She opens up her wallet and shows me pictures of her friends. There are so many, I'm surprised the slender wallet can contain them all.

"My best friend Alicia, she's a quarter Thai and thirty-nine per cent Italian. Ana is Irish, Puerto Rican and ten per cent Cherokee. My boy Armando, his parents are from Afghanistan. His grandmother was born in Egypt."

"What does that make him?" I ask, boiling water for our tea.

"What do you mean?" she says defensively. "He's *American.*"

She looks at me as if I'm crazy.

When I was younger, ethnicity was considered weird. By the time I went to university it was exotic. Now, having a multicultural pedigree seems de rigueur.

I wonder if Tati understands that marketing is behind the latest incarnation of the global-village trend; heritage apparently as easy to replicate in the lab as synthetic chillies and spices. Anyone could be thirty-five parts clever cool corn-chip ad if they really wanted.

"What difference does it make if someone is genetically ninety-nine per cent or two per cent? Hereditary statistics aren't something you flash around like the gold card your mother gave you. There is more to you than just numbers."

Tatiana shoves all the photos back in her purse and doesn't look at me. She knows I'm upset but she doesn't understand why. To tell the truth, neither do I.

I find out later that Auntie Moira is behind the percentages.

My mother's older sister is infamous for many things, but mainly for her penchant for telling tales. Every family has at least one loud-mouthed person who nominates themselves as guardian of rumours and gossip. In our family it was Moira. A weekend holiday in Bahrain once turned into an excursion to an emir's harem. Another time, she worked as an Italian translator for the 1984 Olympics, bewitching the men's swim team with her knowledge of Italian verse.

"But you don't even speak Italian, Auntie," I said.

"Never mind. I recited the great poems of Decamerone. His poems transcend language, Gina."

"You mean Boccaccio."

"No, it was definitely *Decamerone*."

I phone my mother.

"Does Auntie Moira know much about our heritage?"

"She said she was working on a family tree. But you know

my sister. She probably gave it up after a few days." It was no family secret that Mother and her eldest sister didn't get along. "I don't know why Moira is wasting her time. What kind of person wants to dig up kooky old ancestors? It isn't as if they can tell us anything. I mean really, Gina, what good would it do? What's done is done."

My mother baffles me sometimes. She doesn't seem to know or care much about her own family. "An island unto herself" will probably be engraved on her tombstone. I wonder if my mother is adopted as Auntie Moira said she was.

THE NEXT MORNING when Tatiana wakes up, she finds me making a family tree.

"I think this is a perfect project for both of us. What do you think?"

She loves it. She runs to get her markers and pencils and busies herself drawing the tree.

"You're pretty good," I say, admiring her realistic leaves and branches.

"Thanks. I want to study art, but Mom thinks I should do computer science or finance or something." She adds a few more fancy curlicues. "I wonder if anyone in our family was artistic. My mom can't even draw a stick man without making it lopsided."

I tell her my theory of how we humans are like computers with random bits of programming encoded into us. "Some things we recognise – your dad's eyes, say, or your grandmother's nose – but most of your composition is a mystery. For example, why are you so laid back? You didn't get that from your mother."

"I got that from you, Auntie Gina," she says, teasing.

I show her an old box of sepia photos. We look at stern-faced, dark-eyed relatives, searching for similarities, but their stony faces refuse to reveal any secrets. Ancestry.com spits out a long list of possible relations, tenuous connections residing in Korea, Poland, El Salvador, Berlin, Peru, New York, England and Monaco. It will take months to trace them all.

Over the next few weeks we swim, walk, listen to music and work on our family tree. We send out emails like distressed SOSs. We write letters to far-off registrars and subscribe to countless genealogy services.

"This is going to take longer than I thought," I say, when the time comes for Tatiana to leave.

"Yeah," she says, shrugging. "But it was fun. Email if you find anything, you know, *interesting*."

Again, I'm amazed at how important credentials are in her life. It wasn't that long ago that people had to change names, accents, backgrounds, even their hair in order to blend in. Were girls like Tati so tired of the bland homogeneity that they had to hope for, or invent, exotic lineages?

"I'm going to miss you," she says. Standing in my hallway with all her bags she seems smaller, more vulnerable.

"You know you can visit whenever you want, right?"

She hugs me and I watch her get into her mother's SUV. I wave and Chloë touches her hand to her sunglasses like an aviator. I keep waving long after they've turned the corner.

AFTER SHE HAS gone, I continue the quest. I feel it is important for Tati to have a sense of her past, so she can put it aside for a rainy day, proof that she didn't just arrive in the world naked and on her own. Proof she descended from a long line of people connected one to the other. Something larger than just percentages.

But the tree proves difficult. Our lineage has started to resemble a Gabriel Garcia Marquez novel, where all the male relatives are named the same thing over and over again. I realise that digging into one's past is more fairy-tale romance and conjecture than actual history.

I telephone my mother again.

"Why are all the men in our family called Diego, Victor and Antonio?"

"What do you mean, Gina?" I can hear her breathing heavily.

"We are quite the patriarchal family," I say coldly, as if this is all her fault.

"Darling, could you please *try* to be less cryptic? I'm not a mind-reader, you know."

"Mother, could you please stop exercising for a moment? This is serious. How can I track down our ancestors, when the women aren't even in the records by name? Sure, the *paternal* ones are all listed, each with a dutiful little 'wife' designation beside it. But in some cases there's just a question mark, or an 'unknown' written in the box."

"Maybe the names weren't available."

"Then why are the sons from the marriages listed? Six names in some cases! Obviously *someone* took the time to write down *their* details. Why not the female names while they were at it?"

"Not everything is an anti-feminist conspiracy, Gina. Why are you so obsessed with family all of a sudden? You never showed any interest before."

"It isn't for me. It's for Tatiana."

"Tati, huh? Well, it doesn't matter. That's the lesson she should be learning. She's alive and it doesn't matter how she arrived, just that she's here."

"What do you mean, 'it doesn't matter'? Your granddaughter thinks her heritage is a tortilla chip ad!"

"Oh, I like that one. The dancer with the tight trousers is 'hot, hot, hot'."

"*Mother . . .*"

"Gina, honey, sometimes you don't see what's in front of you. It isn't about getting the right dates and names. Those details aren't going to help you solve the mystery of who you are. The important thing is the *story*. You of all people should know that.

She was one to talk, I remember asking her to tell me about my birth. When my mother was pregnant, she firmly subscribed to the martini-martyr-no-pain-mantra of the 70s: a philosophical union of resignation (I have babies, this is what I do), with a predilection for strong prescription drugs and the adamant refusal to suffer while stone-cold sober. She always said she couldn't remember a thing. Now, I pressed for details.

"What was it like? Were you nervous? Were you excited? Were you *scared*?"

My mother ponders these questions for so long my hand starts to get numb from holding the phone. I wonder if I'm being too needy, too pushy, too unfair on her to produce a spectacular and memorable tale. If this had been Moira I would have had what I wanted without even asking.

"Mother, you've just said that details and names aren't what's important. You said it was all about the story. All I want is the story."

"I *was* young," she finally says. "Young and in love and wanting very much to start a family. *Other* women may have been unsure or afraid, but I knew what I wanted. Doctors were only too happy to give us drugs that knocked us out for hours. It was wonderful. You went to sleep and woke up holding a baby. None of this twenty hours of painful, sweaty childbirth nonsense, you see nowadays. Then Lamaze came along and ruined things for everyone. You know back in the time of your great grandmother, they used *chloroform*?"

"But what was the actual experience like? The physical event of it."

"Event? You make it sound like a *party* Gina. Put a bowling ball under your stomach, have it push out of your lady parts and then you'll have some idea. How do *you think* it feels to be ripped apart like that woman in Aliens?"

"Ripley," I say. "She was the heroine and she doesn't get ripped apart. Everyone else does. She's the survivor: proof that women can do it all – kick ass, be smart, look good and still have babies… if they *want* to that is."

I hear her sharp intake of breath and brace myself for what's coming.

"Oh, Gina honey… do you have *something* to tell me?"

"No, Mother. I'm just curious. Can't a person ask a simple question without everyone thinking they're pregnant?"

I scald my tongue on the hot coffee and curse myself for letting her get to me. She's silent on the other line. I say more gently, "Were you in a lot of pain?"

"Christ, yes. It hurt for the first hour like you wouldn't believe, but then Dr. Nicholas put me out of my misery."

(Does one hour even constitute misery?)

"I don't remember anything except feeling sleepy. When I came to I was holding you. The nurses ran out of pink blankets so they wrapped you in a blue one. But everyone could clearly see you were a little girl. You were so cute and helpless: a pretty tiny miracle."

Auntie Moira remembers it differently.

"She was loud and grumpy because the admitting nurses made her take off her jewellery and make-up. You know how sensitive your mother is about her eyebrows," she cackled. "As soon as she came to, she demanded they bring in her cosmetic case, you know the one your father bought her for Christmas. She had it packed to the brim. She even brought the fake wigs and hairpieces! Irma wouldn't let anyone see her until her face was on and the eyebrows returned to their rightful place. Then they brought you out in a boy blanket and she had a fit. Of course in the pictures, you can't see any of that, she looks as she always did. She was wearing a cocktail dress, you know. She told the nurses it was her nightgown and they believed her! Your mother always got her way."

A WEEK LATER I get a package in the post. Baby pictures. My mother, sitting like a queen bee on the hospital bed in a fabulous off the shoulder, see-through peach nightie. Her hair is Pricilla Presley big and her eyes so lined in black velvet; I can barely see her pupils. She is displaying me to the camera, a look of vast achievement and pride and some other emotion I can't make out on her face. I am a bright shade of fuchsia, my eyes scrunched up into Xs, my lips an angry little O. My father sits behind us. He seems small next to my mother, for a man who usually towers over everyone. He is keeping a careful distance, his arms and hands facing inward, as if he is afraid to touch me. My mother tells me this paralytic fear lasted three months.

"You look so young and beautiful," I say when I call to thank her.

"I know," she responds. "I bought that dress in a size bigger than I normally wear. The colour was Iced Champagne. Everyone thought it was gorgeous. I was amazed that I could fit into it straight after giving birth to you. You were such a *large* baby. Of course I regained my figure afterward, but it was never the same." She keeps up a running commentary on her gown that lasts longer than the story of my birth.

"Mother," I say, peering at the picture again. "What happened to your eyebrows?"

"What do you mean?" she snaps, her voice so crisp it crackles the phone line with static. "Look closer. They're right there where they're supposed to be. Listen Gina, are you still working on that family tree? Call my great-uncle Victor. He might be able to help."

GREAT-UNCLE IS EIGHTY-TWO, lives in Paris and is partially deaf in one ear. He used to teach languages and, according to Mother, has a photographic memory. When I call and introduce myself, he has no idea who my mother is. He speaks a strange mixture of Spanish, English and French with a few Latin words thrown in for effect. Over the crackling line, in his monotone multilingual patois, he tells me about my great-great-grandfather.

"Hector was a bit of a character. In his youth, he sowed his oats wildly, as the term goes. Fathered eighteen children. Late in his life he took up with a young married woman from Tripoli – Esmeralda: beautiful, feisty, a real hellraiser." Victor smacks his lips as if he's describing a delicious dish.

"By all reports they had a tempestuous relationship, always at each other's throats, but they still managed to produce six children. Eventually Esmeralda went back to her husband and left Hector with the kids. He was devastated. Kept saying she was the only woman he ever loved. Eventually he found a new woman who took them all in. He died not long after that, but Amelia raised them as if they were her own. You know, Esmeralda showed up on the doorstep some years later wanting the children back, but Amelia wouldn't give them up."

Great-Uncle Victor confesses this last bit to me in a hushed voice, as if the revelation is so shocking it had to be whispered.

"Uncle, I'm so grateful. I haven't managed to get anywhere for months and here you are, a fountain of knowledge. Thank you so much. But how did you know the story about Hector and Esmeralda?"

"Oh, that's easy. Your Auntie Moira told me."

Later, as I sit at my desk with Tatiana's tree, I neatly pencil in Esmeralda's name next to the question mark and wonder how one arrives at percentages.

The Derailment of Anna K

THEY SAY A handshake makes a man. I had been practising mine since the eighth grade, when I clobbered Dagwood Miller 29-8 in the student elections for President of the Junior Council.

"Let's face it, Anna. Girls aren't as good as boys," the little twerp spat as I walked to the front of the school auditorium to accept my victory badge. "You have wimpy limp wrists."

"Oh yeah? You're nothing but a sore loser. I won fair and square, Dag."

"Wimpy limp wrists."

"Sore loser."

"So what if you won? At least I'm not a crybaby girl like you. Girls are weak and stupid."

I shoved him. Hard. So that he went toppling across the stage and crashed into the podium, twisting his ankle and knocking over Mrs Gibbons who was handing out the awards.

"Who is the crybaby now?" I hissed, standing over him as he burst into tears.

Later, in the principal's office – my father and Mrs Gibbons on either side of me and Dagwood, his parents and his bandaged leg on the opposite side of the room – it was decided by all concerned that my unsportsmanlike behaviour should be punished. Dagwood was declared new Student Council President and I was stripped of my badge and demoted to substitute classroom monitor, in charge of cleaning erasers after school.

"Now that we've cleared up that little misunderstanding, why don't you both take a stab at shaking again," said Dr Evans, principal of Greenbay Elementary.

"Go ahead, Anna," said my father.

"Go on, Dag," said Mr and Mrs Miller.

"A good handshake shows you are gracious, even in defeat," said Mrs Gibbons.

"But I won! It was all his fault in the first place. He called me a stupid *girl*."

The entire room turned to glare at me until I stood up and stretched out my hand.

"Fine. OK. Congratulations, Dagwood," I said through gritted teeth.

He gave me a helpless simpering smile. I secretly pretended I was an anaconda squeezing the living daylights out of his hand, but it was no use; he didn't even wince. As he followed his parents out of the room, Dagwood turned and mouthed, "Wimpy limp wrists."

SIXTEEN YEARS LATER and I had cause to crush another slimy-twerp opponent. But this time I was prepared. This time my handshake was as cold and deadly as steel.

His name was Robert Tate, a conventionally handsome thirty-six-year-old former dot-com executive. My company, Miles and Weiss, had recently hired him to fill the gap after we lost our creative director of marketing.

"We are lucky to have him," said the executives at M&W. "Robert Tate is terrifically talented. Comes highly recommended . . . qualified candidate . . . good at sales . . . ruthless when he needs to be . . . a real people person . . . a team player . . . someone who knows how to tell a joke . . ."

Funny? Could tell jokes? Those were the traits they were looking for? I couldn't believe I was being overlooked for some corporate shyster. The last thing our company needed was another clown. What they needed was someone like me.

Any person with half a brain could see that Rob was unsuitable; the shifty type that moved from company to company, always looking out for numero uno and never benefiting any establishment. His résumé showed he had never worked longer than two years at any single place of business, and the closest he had ever come to being creative was a fourteen-month stint auditioning dancers for music videos no one had ever heard of.

"Give me the job. I'm the perfect candidate." I said, "A perfect fit. No one will be as dedicated, loyal or as hard working."

"We hear what you're saying, Anna. We've given it much thought and consideration, but we're going with Rob on this one. By the way, you are doing a great job. Keep it up. Your time will come."

Well trained in the art of corporate politics, I didn't show my disappointment. I didn't jump up and down, push anyone off a podium or accuse my company of being unfair and sexist, although the heartless, manipulative barracudas at M&W deserved it. I swallowed my pride and shook hands firmly with the boys as I'd been taught. Afterwards, I excused myself, went to the ladies' room and made sure the door was locked before allowing myself five minutes of unchecked hysteria.

At the age of twenty-nine, I was already head of new media and business; I had the clout, the advanced degrees, the portfolio of impressive clients, and the energy and ambition to pull it all together. I had been at M&W for ten years, since before graduation, cherry-picked over all my classmates. I was a serious contender, not some hummingbird, fly-by-night wannabe like Rob. Why wasn't I awarded the promotion? I had people skills too.

"Men like to destroy one another," my mother, the prototypical Prozac housewife, used to say, "while women tend to destroy themselves."

She was one to talk. She self-destructed one evening when I was nine, skidding her car into a pond when she was tanked up. She died before the paramedics could rescue her.

I WASHED MY face, applied my lipstick and did my deep-breathing exercises. Then, sitting in a stall with my organiser propped against my knees and high heels pushed against the door, I made notes, attributing my failure to make VP as a combination of the following things: 1. Loss of focus. 2. Loss of killer instinct. And 3. Robert Tate.

"Get rid of Robert Tate," I pencilled neatly in the margins of the page.

DURING THE NEXT day's senior-staff meeting, I took the opportunity to inspect my new boss. He was tall with dark hair and impossibly white natural teeth. Standing in the conference room surrounded by congratulatory colleagues, he appeared poised and unflappable, wearing expensive Italian shoes and a cool, contained smile.

Striding across the room, my black heels clicking on the polished marble floor, I held out my hand and introduced myself. My firm, brisk and impersonal shake was met by a surprisingly soft and squishy hand. Robert's fingers wrapped around mine, holding on for longer than necessary.

Too eager to please, I deemed. Too needy, too keen, too *soft*.

"Welcome," I said crisply.

"Pleased to meet you, Anna. I've heard much about you."

"Well thank you. I've heard a lot about *you* as well."

We smiled politely, sizing each other up. Behind his horn-rimmed glasses, my nemesis' eyes were direct and piercing, like lasers, steel grey with flecks of blue and green. If his handshake was less than VP-worthy, Robert's eyes were in a different class altogether. Despite the roomful of people, we stood locked in a death stare, like grappling gladiators. For a moment, I felt the slightest twinge of apprehension, as if Robert's spotlight eyes could see right through me, right into the heart of my naked ambition. I shivered involuntarily and the moment passed.

"Well, he seems *confident* enough, wouldn't you agree, Anna?" said our boss, the CEO of Miles and Weiss, coming up behind us.

"Let's hope confidence is not his only talent," I said and they both laughed at my little joke.

"Our Anna is one tough cookie," said Mr Miles, chuckling and putting one arm around me and one around Robert as if we were his children. "But don't let her scare you. Here at Miles and Weiss we like to think of ourselves as one big happy family."

"A corporate shyster," my boyfriend Daniel said when I came home that evening and told him about Robert and the cultivated continental arrogance that accompanied the Italian shoes. "He sounds like a man who uses his charm to get what he wants."

"The sort of person that expects you to sit up and take notice. Attention-seeking doesn't even begin to describe him."

"Looks like someone is jealous," Daniel said, putting his arm around me. "Don't be mad. I still swoon when you walk into the room. Doesn't that count?"

"No."

"You have very nice qualities of your own," he said, putting his hand underneath my silk shirt.

"I don't want to be *nice*. I want to be VP."

"Your time will come, honey. Hang in there."

"I've waited long enough. I want it now," I whispered, but Daniel had stopped listening. I tried to concentrate on what his lips and fingers were doing, but I was lost in my own reverie, falling with each breath into a sea of steel grey the colour of eyes.

Later, when Dan was asleep, I turned on the lamp by my side of the bed and worked out a risk analysis on Robert. I based it on information I'd found on the Internet and his résumé and personnel file. The personnel file was tricky to obtain although Lars, the personnel manager, had had a crush on me for years. I went to his office one evening after everyone had gone home. He was busy bending over the printer so he didn't see me walk in.

"What are you doing?" he said. "Step away from that filing cabinet. Those are confidential."

"I need to see Tate's file," I said.

"Oh, sorry, Anna. I didn't recognise you in the dark."

"Could I have a quick look? I won't tell a soul, I swear."

"You know it's against the rules." He adjusted and readjusted his glasses. "I can get fired for something like that."

"I know," I said, walking over to his computer. "I wouldn't ask if I didn't need it. It's important."

"How important?" Lars said, staring at my breasts brazenly.

"Are you done leering?"

"I wasn't . . ."

"Don't. I don't have time for this." I moved over to the filing cabinet and pulled out Rob's folder.

"You can't do that, Anna."

"How are you going to stop me?"

"I'm serious, Anna. I'll tell Mr Tate."

"OK, and I'll tell Hotpants Henderson, your boss, that you've been spending your late-night hours at work wanking off to porn."

Lars turned red and ran to turn off his screen.

"Too late. I've already seen all I need. Don't ever try messing with me, kid. You will lose," I said, tucking the file under my arm and walking out of his office.

ATTENTION-SEEKING MEN LIKE Robert were a dime a dozen and predictable to boot. They relied on a combination of looks, charm and smooth-talking to get what they wanted. Once Rob ingratiated himself with the top brass, he would dole out his time, doing little or no work and planning his next move. Before anything was really expected of him, he would be on to the next big thing, a forgotten blip on our radar. Then I would take the position that was rightfully mine.

I suppose I could have been patient, waiting for him to leave on his own, but I wanted him out as soon as possible. My plan was in simple segments: trust, friendship, seduction, deception and, finally, humiliation and heartbreak. Seduction was a little predictable and old-fashioned but, properly applied, it was highly effective; nothing shattered a man's ego faster than a disastrous affair. But it had to be more than just sex. Mr Handsome probably received enough offers anyway. If I wanted to win this, I needed to go beyond the physical and penetrate the core; expose Robert's essence.

Ironically, until now, I had made a point of keeping my professional reputation as pure as handmade soap. The tawdry affairs of so many of my co-workers repulsed me. What was the point, when you still had to work together once it inevitably ended? Office entanglements could only lead to professional suicide – especially for women. I'd already seen far too many female colleagues fall by the wayside, trampled by ridiculous naïvety and foolish displays of inappropriate emotion. Men, despite their talk of equality, never seemed to be under the same rigorous scrutiny. From where I sat, it was still a man's world and a woman's fall from grace was an Olympian event; people lined up and paid to see. Even a detached person like me – who knew how to keep her mouth shut and her personal life private – had to perch precariously on the gender ladder for fear of falling off. To ensure I never found myself in those situations, I shunned staff parties, drank water at corporate seminars and avoided hotel bars during business trips.

It bothered me a little that I was going to have to utilise my womanly wiles in order to destroy my adversary, especially as I had made such a point of not doing so in the past. But this was war, and all was fair, as the saying went. If I thought it would further my career, I would eat glass if I had to.

WE BUMPED INTO one another a few days later near the fax machine.

"Anna, how are you? I'm so sorry we haven't had a chance to meet and have a formal one-to-one yet."

"Don't worry about it. I know you must be busy. I trust everything is going well?"

"Yes, excellent. Great bunch of people. Lots of new names and faces to remember, though."

"Well, it's only been a few days. Give it time. You'll know everyone's birthday and pets' names by next week."

He laughed. "I hope so. I can't afford to make enemies. Listen, are you doing anything this afternoon? Let me take you out to lunch. Do you like sushi?"

"Love it."

"Great. Is fifteen minutes too soon?"

"Perfect. Meet you outside."

Back at my desk, I quickly applied a slash of scarlet to my bottom lip. Normally pale, the reflection in my compact showed a flushed woman, looking slightly frazzled. It simply wouldn't do. Taking a suggestion from *Cosmo*, I dumped two trays of ice cubes from the corporate kitchen into the bathroom sink, and immersed my face and hands into the icy water until my teeth were chattering. When I was finished, my skin was as cool and smooth as alabaster. My lips on the other hand were blue. I hid it with a generous coating of lipstick.

The restaurant was crowded and the tables so close together our knees were practically touching. I took full advantage of the opportunity, sliding closer and smiling apologetically whenever my leg rubbed against Robert's. Only five minutes and he already looked flustered and nervous. Good, I thought, subtly opening the top button on my blouse. I was on the right track.

We ordered a carafe of sake and a pot of green tea.

"Anna," he said, fixing me with his laser eyes, "can I be honest with you?"

"Of course."

"I mean sincere and completely honest, not just politely honest."

I raised my eyebrows.

"I get the impression you don't like me."

"What? Where did you get that idea?"

"Just the way you stared at me when we first met, as if you wanted to gouge my eyes out."

"Well, you are completely mistaken, Robert."

"Am I? Look, Anna, I know there is some residual bitterness

about this whole VP situation, but I'm not the enemy. I hope you understand that. If this were my company, I would have promoted you over me any day, but the decision wasn't mine to make."

"Somehow, I don't quite believe that. How could you choose me, someone you barely know, over you, whom you have known for, I would like to think, a long time?"

"I know more about you than you think."

"Oh?"

"I know about the foster homes and how you emancipated yourself at the age of sixteen, for example."

"I'm not sure I'm comfortable with the way this conversation is heading," I said, standing up and knocking over the pot of tea. A waitress materialised out of nowhere and sopped up the liquid with a sponge.

"Please sit down, Anna. I'm not going to apologise for reading your personnel file. I can say with almost one hundred per cent certainty that you've read mine. Shortly after meeting you in the boardroom, I realised you weren't like the other stiffs shaking my hand and smiling hypocritically. There was something different about you."

"Considering those stiffs are mostly male and boring beyond belief, I would be highly disappointed if you hadn't noticed."

"Anna, I know you didn't get this far in your career by being just a pretty face. I certainly didn't get this far by playing the fool. So let's get down to brass tacks, shall we? I respect you. With your drive and ambition you will go a long way, but if you think for a moment that I am going to slide over and let you have your way, or become a tragic pawn in some ill-realised scheme, you can just forget it. If you want to hold a grudge, I can't stop you. I would probably do the same. As I see it we have two choices. We can spend all our time trying to stab one another in the back, or we can just acknowledge that we're more alike than we think."

He reached over, poured a cup of sake for me and a cup of tea for himself.

"I know that we probably can't be friends, and that is a shame. From what I've seen, I like you. But as that is unlikely, the least we can do is to spend time getting to know one another. It will make working together easier, don't you think?"

"One of the first things I learned in business was never to underestimate my opponent. I guess in my eagerness and haste to pulverise you, I forgot."

Robert threw back his head and laughed.

It wasn't my nature to be as direct and as sincere as he was pretending to be. But I knew when the game was up. I'd been caught. I took it in my stride and moved on; that was the way to do it. Plus, confessing to having made a mistake had the added benefit of making me more human in Robert's eyes. Later, when I was alone, I would re-evaluate.

"There is something seriously wrong with always dancing to the rhythm of your own ambition," Robert said, putting a piece of sashimi in his mouth. "Going from day to day, stabbing people in the back to rack up brownie points, that's no way to live. And the hours, all that time plotting and planning, spending every hour thinking about how to get ahead. Do you ever ask yourself if there is a point? I mean, look at the things we are willing to do to get to the top. Sometimes I long to be less hungry, less cut-throat. I'd like to settle down and find a different career, maybe paint watercolours or work with animals."

I stared at him over the rim of my cup in disbelief. "That's a load of horseshit. You didn't get where you are today by subscribing to that weedy philosophy. A watercolour artist? Give me a break. We make our choices and our sacrifices and live with them, wrong or right, despite what anyone else says. That's the kind of people we are."

For a moment he looked angry and then a sudden memory of something painful flashed across his face. I was afraid I had gone too far and said something I wasn't supposed to. But after a few seconds he laughed and said that I was right; one ex-wife and a line of countless bitter girlfriends were proof that I was right.

Having had my own struggle with loved ones, I understood better than he knew.

When I was nine years old I launched my first entrepreneurial endeavour: charging neighbourhood kids ten cents an hour to play in my tree house. We had just moved to Seattle, to a house with a huge garden that my father designed himself. The tree house had a hammock, a skylight and a balcony, and the windows opened up to face a nearby lake. It had a loft for my futon, a mirrored vanity area for my play make-up and hairbrushes, and a desk and beanbag chair where I did my homework. It was spectacular. There was also a swinging rope, a climbing wall, monkey bars and a slide. Not in the slightest bit interested in athletic pursuits, I didn't use that part of the tree house.

I had made about twenty-two dollars on my venture before one of the kids told his parents I had taken all his money. My father sat on the corner of the futon and told me he was disappointed that instead of friends I had made clients. He wouldn't stop me from doing what I was doing, but he hoped that on my own, I would see that making money wasn't everything.

Meanwhile, his solution was to take ten per cent of my earnings, which was only fair, he said, as he had made the damned thing and if I was going to be charging admission, he deserved his share.

I was certain that this was a tactic to get me to rethink what I was doing. So to make up for his commission fee, I increased the price of admission from ten to fifteen cents an hour and focused on getting the kids to stay longer. In the end, even my father had to admit defeat. Of course he didn't actually have the chance to admit anything. He fell out of the tree house one day when he was adjusting one of the ropes, slipped and went head first two storeys down. After that I was moved around from foster home to foster home. I didn't fit in with any of the families I stayed with, but unlike some of the other kids I knew, I didn't spend my time rebelling and causing trouble. I learned what I had to do to survive. It sounded harsh to anyone who hadn't been through it, but my experiences taught me a lot about life versus expectations and getting what you really wanted.

AFTER LUNCH, ROB and I stood side by side under the awning of the restaurant, watching the rain and waiting for the valet to bring around our cars.

"Anna," he said, "I know it is hard to let your guard down, even for a moment, and especially with someone like me. But I swear I will do everything in my power not to make things harder for you. Who knows, maybe in a few months I'll be headed elsewhere and then you will get exactly what you want." He turned to face me and his laser eyes were soft as denim. He held out his hand and I took it.

This time, his grip wasn't weak or squishy; it was surprisingly strong.

THREE MONTHS LATER and Robert was well ensconced in his role of VP and showing no signs of wanting to move on. As the weeks flew by, with the promise of spring just around the corner, we continued to adhere to our office peace treaty. We were polite to one another, didn't cut each other down during meetings and occasionally, if we bumped into one another in the hallway, we traded polite smiles. But he didn't leave.

It was time to put my new plan into motion.

One morning when Daniel stayed over, he stopped to sniff

my neck on his way out. "You smell nice. What's the special occasion?"

"No reason. Just felt like it."

"You aren't wearing perfume for some other man, are you? You aren't doing it for that idiot, Robert?"

For some inexplicable reason, his comment made me angry. I pushed him away and went up to the bedroom to finish dressing.

"I was kidding," he called from the bottom of the stairs. "Why are you so touchy lately, Anna?"

"Can't a woman feel pretty now and then without her boyfriend thinking she's having an affair?" I shouted down.

I had never thought of Daniel as the jealous type. We had a relaxed, casual and uncomplicated relationship; no questions asked and certainly no possessiveness. Recently, however, he had begun pushing the boundaries, making pointed comments and acting suspicious. I had enough to deal with at work, without needing that sort of macho posturing in my personal life. I vowed to have a talk with him soon.

THAT EVENING, I casually strolled into Robert's office after work and asked if he wanted to have a drink. We went to a place nearby that specialised in martinis. It was packed to the rafters with business types, their ties loosened and their work shoes abandoned underneath the tables.

A pretty barmaid came by to take our drinks. Even in the dim lighting, I could tell she was entranced by Robert.

"Do you always have this effect on women?" I asked, stirring my drink.

"I don't know what you mean," he said, looking slightly embarrassed.

"Of course you do. You know just how to look at someone and make them feel as if they are the only person in the room.

That's a hell of a talent. You shouldn't be modest about it. I wish I had a power like that. I would be unstoppable."

"I think you underestimate your own powers, Ms Kildare."

"Are you speaking from personal experience?" I took a sip of my vodka giblet and gave him my most mysterious smile.

My mobile phone chose that moment to go off.

"Excuse me for a moment," I said, heading towards the ladies' room.

"What is it, Daniel?" I snapped. "I'm in the middle of something. I'm working late tonight."

"We had dinner plans," he said quietly.

"Sorry, I've just been so busy for the last few days. Work up to my ears. Unfortunately, it isn't something I can get out of easily."

"Anna, we've been planning this for weeks. We had reservations and you know Mario's has a six-week wait."

"I know. I'll make it up to you another time, I promise."

"Another time? It is my birthday. When will you make it up to me? Next year? Will you have time for me next year, Anna?"

I closed my eyes and rested my cheek against the cool white tiles.

"I'd be there if I could. I really would. Why don't we postpone the champagne until tomorrow? I promise I won't lift a single file, won't think about work once."

"No, it's too late now. You enjoy yourself tonight. Don't worry about me. You know, you want me to care, but you want me to care on your own terms. I can't do this any more."

"Don't be like that, Danny."

"Oh, is it *Danny*, now? Anna . . ." He paused. "Be careful. You're playing a dangerous game and someday you are going to slip up."

"Daniel –"

Click. I snapped my mobile shut, put it into my handbag and turned to look at my reflection in the mirror. I didn't have any ice this time, but I pushed my face against the cold-water tap until it started to tingle. Then I applied another coat of lipstick. The blue underneath was starting to show through, making my lips look violet.

When I returned to our table, Robert was waiting.

"Everything OK?"

"Yes, fine. No problem," I said. I flashed him a big smile, but my temples were starting to pound, a sure sign that one of my famous migraines was due any moment.

"Would you excuse me again?" I ran to the bathroom, popped two codeine and was back before he had a chance to reply. "Now, where were we?"

"Well, I was just saying I'm sorry but I have to cut this short. I have an early meeting tomorrow with Miles. But I hope you feel better soon."

My look of surprise must have been evident.

"The little vein in your temple," he said, reaching over and touching me lightly on the forehead. "I can see it pulsing. You need to go home and lie down in a dark room."

I nodded.

"See you tomorrow at work, Anna." He put some money on the table and was gone.

"Where did your friend go?" asked the barmaid when she came to collect the bill.

I gave a dismissive wave.

"Oh, that's a shame. You two weren't, like, together, were you?"

"What's it to you?" I snapped, grabbing my change and

not bothering with a tip.

"Sorry, jeez. I was just asking. What a bitch," she said as she walked away.

I got home before the migraine started. When I arrived, the house was quiet with no sign of Daniel. I went into the bedroom and noticed the few shirts and suits he had in my closet had disappeared. In the living room his CDs and books were gone. In the kitchen I found an empty bottle of champagne with a photograph of the two of us at a New Year's Eve party propped up against the side. Daniel's arm was around my waist and I was leaning into him, smiling happily for the camera. I tore it neatly in two halves down the middle and threw one into the bin. The other I put on the stainless-steel refrigerator, held up by a Miles and Weiss magnet.

I took a long hot bath and went to bed.

ONE MONDAY AT 9 p.m. when we were both working late, Robert came in to ask my opinion on an upcoming report.

"It looks like someone hasn't been doing their homework." I did a pyramid-of-power thing with my hands.

"Anna, please don't do that. You look like my old school principal."

"Miles is going to flip when he sees that report."

"Do you think it can be rescued?"

"How much time do we have?"

"It has to be in by the end of this week." He grimaced.

"Robert, I'm in the middle of preparing for the Avis presentation."

"I completely understand. But this needs to be done ASAP, Anna. Avis can wait. Look, I wouldn't ask if I wasn't over my head." His grey eyes looked serious.

"Fine. I'll see what I can do. Leave it on my desk. I wish

you had told me sooner. It isn't going to be stellar, but I'll take a stab."

"Thanks, you're a lifesaver. Don't worry. I trust you to do a great job. I owe you one."

"And I'll make sure you pay up."

He smiled and closed the door softly as he left my office.

Great. I had him right where I wanted him. I hoped he would stay meek and pliable, at least for a little while. Rob was grateful now, but I suspected he was like all the others. He would turn around, quick as a slithering snake, and bite my hand the first opportunity he had.

It took me over thirty-five hours to finish the report. On Friday, I left it on his desk at 8:00 a.m. and when I returned to mine, there was a bottle of wine and flowers in my office. White freesias. I closed my eyes and inhaled their clean, fragrant odour. It had been a long time since anyone had given me flowers.

In the evening Robert was whisked off by the partners, having successfully wooed them with my report. I wondered if I had done the right thing by helping him. Would he have helped me out of a jam? Probably not. Still, it was done. If that hadn't proved my trustworthiness, nothing else would. I sat in my office sorting out paperwork until after 10:00 p.m..

When I walked out to my car, Robert was in the parking lot, leaning against his car door, waiting. "Nice night," he said.

"Have you been waiting long?"

"Not really. Anna, you have no idea how much your help meant to me. They loved it. Everyone was really impressed. I took Miles aside and told him about your contribution. I told him how amazing I thought you were."

"Oh?" I said.

"I'm being serious. I wanted him to know how much work you put into it."

I stood rooted to the concrete, wondering if I should believe him. "Well, you can pay me back when I need it," I finally said.

"Right. You don't need my help. You don't need anyone's help."

Our cars, the only two left, sat together side by side, gleaming expectantly in the empty lot.

"I guess a celebratory drink is out of the question?"

"Sorry, I'm shattered. I need to get home."

"Anna, do you realise how compatible, how in synch we are?" Robert placed his hand on my arm before I could open my door.

"Have you been drinking, Rob?"

"Yes – I mean no. I mean, the usual amount. I'm not drunk if that's what you are getting at. I only had a few drinks. Please hear me out . . . I've been giving this a lot of thought. We are compatible. This sort of rapport doesn't just happen every day. We are committed, devoted and passionate about our work. But most importantly, and I know this might sound silly, but I feel we are *connected*. I'm not sure how appropriate it is to say that in our situation. I don't know if I should be saying anything at all. The only thing I'm certain of – the only thing I know – is that I'm totally in awe of you at this moment."

The glow of the full moon illuminated us from above like a spotlight. For a moment, I felt like Ingrid Bergman in *Casablanca*.

As if on cue, a gust of wind swept a strand of hair across my forehead.

"Beautiful," Rob said, looking up at the sky. "Absolutely beautiful."

I wanted to ask if he meant the moon or me, but before I had the chance, he leaned in and kissed me lightly. His mouth tasted sweet and salty and bitter. I closed my eyes and moved towards him, but he pushed away just as suddenly as he had kissed me. He shook his head and without saying a word, got into his car. I hoped he would turn around or roll down the window and say something. But he didn't. He sped off into the night, leaving me standing alone in the parking lot. I tried not to shiver as the cool night air hit my skin, and when the rain started pouring, I stayed rooted for a few moments before taking cover in my car.

AT LUNCHTIME THE next day, I saw Rob in the cafeteria buying soup. Our eyes met briefly before he turned away to sit with a group of colleagues from Sales. I sat by myself at one of the tables with a sandwich and a paper.

A few days after that we had a staff meeting. I occasionally caught Robert's sharp eyes sweeping the room like searchlights. In case it was me he was looking for, I avoided contact, keeping my eyes on my organiser and doodling sketches in the margins.

The following week, I saw him in the hallway but he pretended not to see me.

It was time to call in the big guns.

MR MILES WALKED into my office and shut the door. I didn't even look up from the whiteboard where I was preparing notes for the next day's meeting.

"So, to what do I owe this honour?" he said, coming up behind me and placing his hands on my hips. "You smell wonderful, by the way," he said, snorting my neck like I was hiding truffles under my hair.

"What do you mean?"

"You called me earlier and left a message saying you needed to speak urgently. You know I've always said I would be willing to help, but don't play silly games, girl. I don't have time for it." His hand reached down inside my suit jacket.

"Stop it. I'm working. Miles, someone is going to see us."

"Let them. Besides, everyone's gone home already."

I knocked his hand away. "I didn't call you here for that."

"Come on, you can't still be mad at me about the promotion. I explained it to you. If you don't trust me, that is your business. I had nothing to do with it. You would think after all the years we've known one another, you'd know better."

His cold fingers moved inside my blouse. I closed my eyes and tried not to cringe. I knew I was treading on dangerous ground, but it wasn't something I couldn't handle. Miles had made it clear to me from the first day I started at M&W that if I wanted something from him, all I had to do was ask *nicely*. Even now, I was reluctant to call in a favour, especially since I had told him many times that this wasn't how I operated. I wanted to work my way up to the top like everyone else. Now here I was with my CEO's shrivelled liver-spotted hand inside my blouse.

Despite what Miles said, I knew he sold me out with the VP business. I had no reason to think he would be on my side. The only thing I had was a strong hunch that the pervy old bastard liked to seduce his female employees.

"I need a favour," I said, cutting straight to the chase.

"Ah, back to that, are we? Do you think you are the only one who has desires, Anna?" Miles said, drooling into my ear. "We all have motives. You want something, I want something. We are in a position to help one another. It is an ugly truth that when all the pretty fancy words and concepts are swept aside, all you are left with is nothing more than supply and demand. That's business in a nutshell, stripped of all its glamour." He ground his knee against my pelvic bone. "Now, do we do this the easy way, or the way I like it?"

It figured that Miles would consider his supply-and-demand speech as foreplay. The old man never changed his tune.

"I would love nothing more. But not right now."

He frowned and looked at his watch. "Couldn't we just . . . very quickly . . . right here?" He pointed at his trousers and I had to stop myself from shuddering.

"No. If you wait, I promise I'll make it worth your while." I put his wrinkled hand under my skirt, so he could feel the clasps of my stockings. "You wouldn't want to spoil the surprise, would you?"

"When?" he said, panting so hard I thought he was going to die of a heart attack in my office.

"A few nights from now. My place."

"No. If you want something from me, it has to be here. Right now." He pushed me hard against my desk.

"Fine, let's do it your way, then." I unbuttoned my shirt to reveal a black bustier underneath. I had heard through the office grapevine that our CEO had a thing for lingerie.

Miles took a sharp intake of breath.

"But first . . . I need a favour."

"Can't it wait, Anna?"

"No. Fair is fair, you said so yourself."

"What do you want?" he said, tugging at the zipper on my skirt.

"It's Robert Tate."

"What about him?"

"He needs to go."

"Anna, we've already been through this."

"No, not really."

"Do we have to do this now?"

"Yes."

"What's in it for me?"

"Anything you want."

Miles stopped fumbling with my clothing. "Anything?"

"Whatever you want."

He yanked my skirt up brusquely; I heard the material rip.

"Tate is harmful to the organisation. He doesn't know how to keep his mouth shut. There's been talk."

"Oh?"

"Quite a bit, apparently. He knows about you and that intern you hired last year."

"How did he find out?"

"I guess Lois at reception was unhappy and ran to him with it. He confided it to me the other night over drinks."

"Why would he tell you?"

"I guess he was trying to get something out of it."

"So, what do you think we should do?"

"Get rid of him. He is a rotten apple. He's only going to spread bad feelings around. You don't need that, especially after the way William left."

Miles stopped what he was doing. "You knew about that?"

I nodded. "Don't worry, I didn't tell anyone."

The CEO of Miles and Weiss had taken me under his wing when I was younger. Our relationship was strictly platonic and Miles was like a father to me. Once a month he took me to lunch and we would exchange information. As a watcher and a student of intuition, I was perfectly positioned to deliver him morsels of knowledge, hand-feeding them to my boss as if he was my lover. I revealed all the gossip: who was crumbling, who was weak, who he should watch out for and use to his advantage. In turn he gave me advice, told me how to proceed in certain situations and how hard to push. Eventually I found

I no longer needed him. I had grown strong enough to manage on my own. It had been a long time since he had taken me into his confidence.

"Can I trust you on this, Anna?"

"Absolutely."

He pulled my face towards him.

"If I find you are lying to me, it will be your head first, before his. Got that?"

"I'm telling you the truth."

"Fine. I can't guarantee anything – he's well liked at the moment. But I'll do my best. That's all I can promise. Now, you and I have something to finish."

Miles may have been old, but he was far from senile and still as sharp as ever. I was hoping for a little more than just a vague promise. Never mind. I wasn't going to give up so easily. I would whisper in his ear while he was banging me, every night if I had to. Eventually, some of it would start ringing true. I closed my eyes and tried to ignore what he was doing, thinking of Robert and his grey eyes, which were so deep I wanted to drown in them. Perhaps in other circumstances we could have had a chance. Now I would never know. If we were so alike, he would have no problem understanding why I did what I did.

"Tell me how much you want me," my boss demanded, panting away behind me.

I put the image of Robert and his eyes out of my mind and told Miles what he wanted to hear. I played my part so effectively, in fact, that I almost managed to convince myself.

THE LITTLE MAN

I'D INVITED VERONICA to accompany me to the 7th Annual Conference for the Midwest Seed Growers of America. Over a leisurely room-service breakfast, I sat in my bathrobe, spreading cream cheese on a bagel and enjoying one of those rare moments of contentment that doesn't require conversation or synchronised activity. Veronica sat on the corner of the bed, brushing her hair and watching a television programme about cosmetic surgery.

"Jules, do you think I need a *boob* job?" she asked, cradling her perfect breasts in her hands. "What do you think? You know when gravity takes its toll these *puppies* will be the first to suffer. No one, absolutely no one is going to want to hire a model with saggy boobs… *HEY*, are paying attention?"

After months of sending her portfolio around, Veronica had finally landed an audition at the Home Shopping Channel. Her dream had always been to work in television, but I told her she was far too talented for a place that forced her to smile like a simpleton while modelling imitation gold necklaces.

The Home Shopping Channel was just a stepping-stone on the ladder of her success, she said in an irritated voice. Later, she'd move on to better things: car commercials, toothpaste ads, game shows, maybe even the news someday.

"I'm still young, you know, *Jules*."

How could I forget? Veronica was always reminding me of how young she was.

"I told you I hate it when you call me Jules."

"Fine. *Julian* then. Why are you ignoring me, *Julian*? What are you reading that's so important?" She jumped on my side of the bed and snatched the itinerary from my hands. "You made a schedule for today? I thought the point of this trip was for us to be together."

"No. The point of this trip is *work*."

Whenever Veronica got upset, her face stayed passive but her voice dropped note by note until it reached Antarctic temperatures. She also had the unfortunate habit of over-emphasising random words, as if she'd grown up watching a pissed-off Captain Kirk on Star Trek. "You said you *weren't* going to *attend* the stupid *conference*. What was the *point* of asking me to come along?"

Not all my time was devoted to Veronica, you understand. Well, not as much as she would have liked. In my spare hours, I liked to fashion things out of natural fibres; sculptures, I guess you could call them. I loved the feel of mud on my hands: good, red, country clay instead of plaster. I enjoyed painting and drawing as well, and was eager to visit Chicago's famed museums, which I had heard so much about.

I'd carefully worked out a schedule that allowed me time to network with colleagues, do some sight-seeing and still spend time with Veronica.

"There isn't anything *exciting* on here," she said, shoving the itinerary away as if it repulsed her. "It's all *museum* this, architecture that. If you were planning to go to museums and *stuff*, why did you bother to *bring* me along?"

"I thought we could enjoy them together, Veronica."

"Fat chance. Can't we do anything fun?"

There was that word again. *Fun*. She had been using it against me like a silver bullet for the past few months: "You're no fun, *Jules*. Why aren't you any *fun*. You never let me have any *fun*. When I met you, you used to be so much *fun* . . ."

"Look, Veronica, a little bit of culture won't kill you."

She narrowed her eyes.

"Please, let's not fight today."

"You think I need more *culture*?"

I remained silent.

"You think I'm not educated like you, that I don't *know* things? Well, I *know* plenty of things. I may not be a *la-dee-da* artist, but at least I'm not a *hick* farmer like you."

"I'm not a farmer, Veronica. I told you: I sell farming equipment. I'm a *distributor*. Maybe all that hair brushing is affecting your grey cells."

"You can be a real *jerk*, you know that, *Jules*?"

She went back to the mirror to continue the inspection of her breasts. She turned this way and that, huffing like an angry mare, preening and posing and lifting her delicate hoofs.

After a few minutes she calmed down a little and looking over her shoulder to make sure I was watching, she arranged herself into my all-time favourite pose. With her swan neck elongated, and her slender back arched, her auburn hair tumbled over her shoulders and fell down to her full buttocks.

Strategically positioned near the window, the morning sun bathing her in its golden light, every inch of Veronica's skin appeared luminous and alive. She could be difficult and extremely vain but, God, she was beautiful.

"Come here, darling," I said in a thick voice. "I think I have something *fun* we can both do."

IT WAS HER flawless beauty that first captivated me. I was enchanted, then, later, obsessed, by the red-haired woman with the creamy skin that seemed almost unreal, like something made of wax.

Veronica worked as an artist's model for one of my life classes. Week after week she sat naked, arms behind her head, legs outstretched on the dais, as we attempted to capture the angles of her limbs, the fleshiness of her curves. She had the uncanny ability to mimic a statue perfectly. Her marble limbs held the poses like a Greek goddess. The art students never ceased to be amazed and delighted by her modelling, and no one more than me.

As the semester progressed, I purposely began to search her out. I arrived at class earlier and earlier, in hope of catching her doing ordinary things: eating, or wearing her own street clothes. Did she wear little skirts that showed off the symmetry of her toned legs or long ones that brushed against her calves? Did she prefer low-cut tops that hugged her ample assets or faded sweatshirts? It was strange; I had seen her naked so many times that I now fantasised about seeing her clothed.

On the one occasion I was successful, I watched Veronica wander into the studio eating an apple and wearing blue jeans. I was so excited; I could barely contain my pleasure. I made a mental note of how she sat at the back of the empty classroom, glancing nervously towards the door, as if at any moment the students would march in and find an intruder occupying their space.

I began seeking her out more boldly during classes. I purposely didn't avert my eyes, staring even after she put on her robe and stepped back into the makeshift dressing room. A few times during our sessions, I thought I noticed her flicking her eyes in my direction, just the smallest shift and then back to her usual statue-like self. I felt a thrill from these brief moments of imagined contact. Often these meagre interactions between us were the highlights of my week.

We carried on this way for some time. I grew crazier and crazier about her with each passing day but I was too afraid to say anything. Then one day I found her waiting for me after class. Standing outside of the classroom with her hair pulled back, Veronica, up close and in person, was far better than the frozen goddess of my dreams. I barely managed a hello, but she smiled and invited me to sit with her over a cup of coffee.

"I hope you don't mind me saying, but you're a little old to be a student," she said.

"Yes, well, you know what they say: you're never too old to learn new tricks."

She laughed and told me she never went to college. She was too busy working. At the moment she was holding down three jobs: waitressing at a coffee house near the campus, stacking books at the library and working as a life model.

"I need to pay for elocution lessons. What I really want to do more than anything is model. You know, for magazines and stuff."

"I'm sure you will get there one day," I said.

"You think?"

"Absolutely. You are very striking and that's not a pick-up line. I'm being honest. I could see you in the pages of a magazine. Like the J. Geils song."

"Jay who?"

"Never mind. Another lifetime ago."

"I'm not tall enough to be a *fashion* model. I'm only five foot nine. But I can do commercial work. I heard on some gigs you even get to keep the clothes."

"I'm sure some agency will snap you up. You're a knock-out."

"Thanks. I *like* you, Julian. You have a nice face. You remind me of someone I used to know."

She smiled and sipped her black coffee and I smiled right

back. But inside my stomach was churning, wondering who I reminded her of. I wasn't one for comparisons.

After that, Veronica waited for me on Tuesdays at the café around the corner from the studio. Before I knew it, we were engaged in a game of harmless flirting: nothing serious, just a little fun. But the more time we spent together, the more intense it became. Veronica was like a languid cat, stretching out her long body against the diner booth until she was practically on my lap. I would carry on with the conversation, pretending she had no effect on me. I thought perhaps she was testing me, waiting to see if I only wanted her for her perfect body and not her mind. On other occasions, she would apply and reapply her cherry lipstick, looking at me and licking her lips, even though the gloss kept rubbing off on her coffee cup. I had to constantly remind myself of the dangers of lusting after young women. For God's sake, she had just turned nineteen and I was pushing fifty-four!

But some things can't be helped.

Veronica drew me the way the moon draws water and I was helpless, completely besotted when I was around her.

OUR MORNING TOGETHER at the Field Museum was a quiet one. I wasn't sure if that was due to our fight or because the surroundings called for it, but Veronica was particularly reserved. I attributed it to her resentment at being dragged along against her will. I had promised we would do some shopping afterwards and she agreed reluctantly, on the condition that we wouldn't spend too much time getting "cultured" as she called it. We walked through the galleries without speaking or holding hands, only stopping to look at the displays she found interesting. She ignored the Neanderthals, witch doctors and totem poles. But as we turned the corner at Mesoamerican Artefacts, she finally came alive.

"Look at all this gold!"

I smiled like a doting parent. I had a particular passion for the art of the pre-Columbian period myself.

Her eyes took in the collection of bracelets, rings and earrings displayed on the velvet cloth. "Imagine wearing this," she breathed, her eyes round like agates. "'The Necklace of Promises. Worn by the Princess Q'tante on her wedding day.'"

I walked up behind Veronica as she leaned over the case. The necklace she was looking at was impossibly heavy – a chain of braided gold links and intricate weavings that resembled an elaborate dog collar. At each end was a clever mechanism of interlinking twists that locked together like a puzzle.

The Necklace of Promises was designed by the Warrior Prince Tezomoc for his bride. The clasp symbolised unity between the two royal families, and the criss-crossing pattern on the chain represented the long road of honour and duty. As tradition dictated, the necklace was placed on the bride's neck during a private ceremony. Once locked, it was locked for eternity and could never be taken off, even in death.

"The princess had to wear that thing forever?"

"Maybe she was flighty," I said, spanning my hands around Veronica's neck. "Maybe the prince was afraid she would be unfaithful. You have to admit it's a good way to keep your wife under lock and key."

"You know what?" she said. "You're not a very nice person sometimes, Julian. *And* you have *trust* issues. You don't think people can be faithful to one another."

"That's not true."

"Yes it is. Your imagination is pretty limited. You don't even believe in eternal love."

"I'll have you know there's nothing wrong with my imagination. I'm imagining you right now, wearing that necklace and nothing else."

"Stop," she said, pushing my hands away.

"Why? Does the thought excite you?" I bit the tip of her ear.

"Julian, cut it out," she said, moving away from me.

Lately she got upset without even needing a reason. She flinched when I tried to touch her and expressed disinterest when I tried to be affectionate. I felt like a skater skimming on the thin ice of her indifference. I suppose she had simply grown tired of waiting for me to commit.

It was true I had issues with trust, but I was working on changing that. Later tonight over a romantic candlelight dinner, I would prove to Veronica how serious I was.

I had been married once before in my 30s: a short-lived relationship with a much younger woman, little more than a kid, really. She was a pretty girl, smart and sweet. We both fell head-over-heels, but it didn't last. Within a year we were divorced.

While Veronica was also young, she was wilful and had a fierce determination my first wife lacked. With my ex, everything was precious and tinged with a bittersweet sense of entropy. I tried to remember how I'd felt about her, but the memory was remote and distant, like an old sepia photo.

Leaving Veronica gawking at the jewellery I moved to another display to look at a collection of silver daggers and obsidian knives. One of the daggers had an emerald-encrusted handle, elaborately engraved with the face of a beautiful woman that resembled a jaguar. It was a superbly crafted piece. It had belonged to Prince Tezomoc, the same man who had designed the Necklace of Promises. I turned to show Veronica, but she was busy leaning against a pillar talking to a man. He slipped into the shadows as I approached them.

"Who was that?"

"Where?"

"That person I saw you talking to."

"What?"

"The man. I saw you with a man."

She rolled her eyes at me as if I were crazy. "The only man I see here is this guy." She signalled to an idol so small he seemed to float in the immensity of his glass case, like one of those plastic deep-sea divers they have in aquariums. Any other object might have looked lost and vulnerable suspended in empty space, but he looked apoplectic, as if he was raging against the unfair confinement of his incarcerated predicament.

"'Aztec deity believed to be the corn god of fertility,'" read Veronica in her Shopping Channel voice. "'Discovered in a cave in 1942, in the province of Gauna . . . Guane . . .'"

"Guanimotoana," I said.

"*Guanimotoana*," she echoed, in the hushed, reverent tones of a Discovery Channel presenter during shark week. "'Researchers have nicknamed him the Little Man.'"

"I can read too, Veronica," I said.

She shrugged. "I like reading out loud. Don't you think I have a good voice?" She put her hand to her windpipe to perform her vocal exercises. "Ah, eh, eeh, oh, ooh. See? I've been practising."

"I wonder why they call him the Little Man," I said.

"Just look at him. Look at his tiny hands. See how they're *bunched* up into fists like he is clutching them in rage? Does he remind you of *anyone*, Julian?"

I leaned in to get a better look at the ugly idol. The display was tucked away in a dark corner, across from the other exhibits.

"I wonder why they've put him here where no one can find him?"

"Maybe he's so special he gets a case all by himself," Veronica said, placing her hands on the glass. "Look at his eyes, Julian. They're absolutely breathtaking."

For some reason she seemed taken with the corn man. From a purely artistic point of view, I found nothing interesting. He seemed crude and badly made, especially in the bleak dimness of the room.

But she was right. Someone had taken great care with the eyes. Different-coloured pieces of turquoise surrounded a larger piece of honey amber. It gave the idol the disconcerting appearance of having pupils.

"You know what I think? He must have been someone special in his time."

"I wouldn't make any assumptions, Veronica. He's probably a common fertility statue."

"No, he's not ordinary. See how he is standing? He's *special*. This little guy was made to be looked at. *I* would know."

I stared at the cornhusk-shaped body, the arms akimbo as if prepared for battle. Despite his ostracised status the Little Man didn't look lonely at all. He looked menacing. Although no bigger than a pencil, his diminutiveness didn't in the slightest reduce his haughty, regal demeanour. The hideous little god glared back at us, his ivory teeth shining in the glow of the halogen light.

"Yes, I can *see* a definite resemblance," said Veronica, looking from me to the Little Man. Her eyes glittered like emeralds in the darkness of the museum.

"Oh, *relax* Jules. I'm just teasing."

I was sensitive about my height, I admit it, but recently my lover had taken on a nastiness that crossed the line from gentle teasing into the realms of playground cruelty. I felt deeply humiliated by her and it wasn't the first time. I pressed my arms to my body, fingers drawn into fists, without realising I was imitating the Little Man.

"'He was found buried face first in an unmarked mound,

under seven layers of dirt,'" Veronica read. "'Bound in dark bandages, his eyes were protected by two golden coins. Legend has it that before the consummation of his royal marriage, Prince Tezomoc, in a fit of jealous fury, murdered his beloved Q'tante on their wedding night.'

"It says here if you look closely you can see the statue wearing a miniature dagger; the patterns of his garb like the ones on the Necklace of Promises.

"You know what? I'm going to take a picture. Jules, why don't you get up close to it and clench your fists again?"

No sooner were the words out of her mouth than a man appeared wearing the beige uniform of a security guard.

"No pictures, please," he said, holding up his hand. "It's against the rules." He gestured to a sign, barely visible in the funereal lighting of the Mesoamerican display.

Absolutely no flash-bulb lighting or photographic equipment allowed in this wing.

"How did you know we were getting ready to take a photo? Were you following us around?"

The guard flushed a deep red. "It's my job to keep an eye on things around here, ma'am."

"Well, it's a little hard to see the sign in the dark," she said. "I was just so taken with this little statue. I don't suppose you'd allow a few quick photos?"

"No, ma'am. I'm afraid that's not possible."

"I understand," she said, pressing her pretty pink lips into a pout.

The guard was tall and muscular, young and handsome with blond hair and a tan. The kind of guy I could imagine Veronica with if she wasn't with me. The problem with having such a beautiful woman as a girlfriend was that you were never safe from the prying eyes of other men. No doubt this poor fool had been lurking in the shadows all morning, watching our every move. Veronica seemed to attract the stalker type.

"Excuse me," said my girlfriend, "but don't you think my *companion* here looks a bit like the Little Man?"

The guard gave me the once over.

I had an urge to punch his perfect chiselled chin.

"See the way he is standing?" she asked.

I scowled at them, my arms at my waist.

The guard nodded and then laughed. They laughed together: Veronica with her head thrown back and her long neck exposed, and blondie with all his perfect white teeth.

"Are you sure I can't take just one picture?"

"Oh, all right, just a quick one," he said. "Just for you, princess."

"What did you call her?" I said.

The guard gave me a strange look.

"Don't worry about him. His bark is worse than his bite." Veronica fluffed up her hair. She was such a shameless flirt.

When he left, she turned to me and shoved her purse in my hands. "Here, hold this," she demanded. She took two pictures of us in quick succession.

"Why did you say that to the guard, Veronica?"

"What does it matter? It worked, didn't it?"

"I wish you would stop comparing me to this thing. It's insulting."

She shrugged and put away her camera.

"Listen, we've been here long enough," I said, looking at my watch.

"No, you go ahead. I'm not done yet. There are a few more things I want to see."

"Like what?"

"I don't know. *Stuff.*"

"I see. So you're going to wait around for your little friend the security guard? Hanging out with him so you can both laugh at me again?"

"Don't be *stupid*, Julian. That was just something I said to distract him. I'm enjoying the museum. That's what you wanted, right?"

"Yes, but I can't believe you are wasting time looking at this piece of junk. Especially when you didn't even want to come in the first place. There are more interesting things to see, like the Aztec chocolate exhibit. Or the Emperor's collection of crowns. You would love that."

"I don't want to see crowns or *chocolate*. Besides, I'm not holding you here. If you want to leave, go," she snapped.

"Come on, leave this ugly corn man," I said, trying to wrap my arms around her.

"No. You go ahead, Julian. I'm going to stay for a bit longer. I need time to think about *things*."

I finally lost my patience. "Think about things? What is there to think about, Veronica? It's a creepy statue. It was found buried in a cave and it's hideous. End of story!"

My voice came out louder than I intended. I had been looking forward to walking hand-in-hand through the museum with her, stopping now and then to kiss on the benches or in the alcoves, and here we were, fighting again.

The security guard put his head around the corner. "Mind keeping it down, folks? You're disturbing the other patrons."

I glanced around the empty room; we were the only people there.

"Sorry, we'll keep it down."

He winked at my sweetheart and disappeared again.

Veronica turned her back to me and sat on the bench. "What's the big deal?" she whispered.

"What, now you don't want to be with me? Is that it? I

don't understand."

"I don't *know*. I need time to think. Stop crowding me."

She flinched as I tried to grab her hand.

"Julian," she said in a low voice, "why don't you go ahead to the chocolate thing by *yourself*? I'll meet you in a few hours. At that *tea* place you like."

"But I thought –"

"Please, I just want to be on my *own* for a few hours." And with that she looked around the room again and took off in the other direction, leaving me standing in the gallery alone.

She had succeeded in humiliating me again. I felt the bile rise in my throat. I swore it would be the last time.

THE CHOCOLATE EXHIBIT turned out to be a big let-down. In fact, the rest of the museum seemed as dead as all its exhibits without Veronica's company. On my way out, I noticed a gift shop with replicas of the museum's collection.

"Excuse me," I said to the pretty blond woman behind the counter.

"May I help you, sir?"

"This necklace, is it an exact replica of the Necklace of Promises?"

"Yes," said the woman. "Would you like to see it?" She lifted it out of its velvet case. "A beautiful handmade piece. See the elaborate workmanship on the gold? Just like the original. Is this for someone *special*?"

"Yes, a gift," I said. "A gift for my *wife*."

"Isn't she the lucky lady," said the blonde.

"I'm the lucky one."

"How *romantic*. I wish my boyfriend would hurry up and propose." Her laugh had a little tinkle.

"Do you really think she will like it . . . *Anne*?" I said, leaning in and reading her nametag.

Anne blushed as if I had asked her to meet me in my hotel room. "It's absolutely gorgeous. She's going to love it. I *guarantee* it."

I SAT IN the Russian Tea Room, fingering the package the shop assistant had thoughtfully tied with red ribbons. Veronica was going to be so excited when she saw it. I imagined her opening the lid, delighted and breathless as a little girl. She would demand that I put it on immediately. I would lift the hair off the back of her neck and lean in to inhale her wonderful musky smell. The smell I had often said she could bottle and sell, if the television thing didn't pan out.

For a brief moment, I considered giving her the Necklace of Promises as a wedding present. I imagined the happiness and surprise on her face.

The first time we slept together; Veronica confessed she'd developed a crush on me in the art classes.

"I found you so attractive, so irresistible, but I couldn't do anything. I'd been warned about talking to people from the class. It could get me fired. One day I saw you staring at me as though I was the best thing in the world, and I knew you felt the same way."

She told me she wasn't in the habit of flirting with students, in case I got the wrong idea about her. She placed her small hand on top of my chest. I felt my skin burn beneath her fingertips, as if seared by the radiance of her touch. I didn't say a word, afraid she would remove her hand and with it my heart.

Despite how she felt, Veronica said it was inappropriate for us to have any kind of relationship. I was too old for her and she wasn't ready for anything serious. As I leaned over to touch her hair and tell her I understood, I noticed she was crying. I pressed my lips lightly to hers to soothe her and then suddenly I was holding her so tightly she couldn't breathe.

Veronica brought something primal out in me. In her arms I discovered what had been missing from my life all these years. I finally knew what it was to love someone with a fierce and devoted passion, and now that I had found her, I was never going to let go.

An hour and forty-five minutes later, I was still waiting for Veronica at the restaurant. I glanced at my watch again and noticed the waiter hovering discreetly with a pitcher of water. I called him over and ordered another whisky.

"Will you be having anything to eat, sir?"

I shook my head brusquely and he took the menus away.

My appetite was now completely spoiled and I was starting to get a migraine. I reached into my jacket and touched the pretty box with the necklace. I liked the sensation of the fragile paper against my fingers. It felt even better to crush it in my hand until I felt it crumple. I poured the amber liquid down my throat in one smooth gulp and ordered another.

I didn't see Veronica again until much later, back at the hotel. I came out of the shower to find her sitting on the bed.

"Where were you this afternoon?" I said, trying to keep my voice even.

"I was at the museum."

"All this time?"

"They stayed open late."

"Veronica, is there something you want to tell me?" I said, putting on a clean shirt.

"No. Now is not the time, Julian. I'm not feeling well."

Concern overtook my anger. "What's wrong, my love?" I said, walking over and taking her hand.

Perhaps it was my imagination but I noticed an odd smell on her: a combination of cigar smoke, drink and something I couldn't place. "So all this time you've been at the museum?" I asked.

"Let go of my hand, Julian. You're hurting me."

"Why don't you tell me the truth, then? What were you really doing?"

"What? Are you crazy? I *told* you. I was in the museum. Jesus, Julian. Why are you staring at me like that?"

"No reason," I said. I released her arm and she headed for the bathroom without another word.

When she emerged a half hour later, her eyes and nose were pink. That's the bad thing about redheads; their colouring is so extreme. Any sort of blush or blotch shows up drastically in their pigment. She was wearing a bathrobe and her hair was wrapped in a towel. She sat on the chair near the bed and began to put on her make-up.

"You should really wear your hair up tonight," I said, coming up behind her. "It enhances your elegant neck."

"I like it down," she said, dotting foundation on her cheeks.

"I bought you something today."

"Oh?" she said, not meeting my eye in the mirror.

I reached into my jacket pocket, pulled out the crumpled package and handed it to her.

"Why is the paper all torn?" She frowned.

"I dropped it and someone trampled on it," I lied, unable to tell her I had mangled it myself while waiting for her to show up at the restaurant.

I could barely contain myself as she slowly took the box from me, tore off the paper and flipped open the case. Unlike my earlier fantasies, Veronica did not throw her arms around me or express her undying gratitude. Instead, she just stared at the necklace.

"It's like the one in the museum," I said, my voice unnatural. "Like the one given to Princess Whatshername."

"I know, Julian. I can't believe you bought me a cursed necklace." She spun towards me, a small flame ignited in her eyes.

"What are you talking about?"

"Cursed, yes. Don't you remember? The prince cursed his wife when he accused her of sleeping with someone else."

"That's a legend, Veronica. A *myth*. Is that what you spent all day doing? Listening to that stupid guard with the cleft in his chin?"

"Why would you say that? I *read it myself*, Julian? I'm not *stupid*. I *can* read, you know. God, I was standing beside you! Don't you remember?"

I felt dizzy, so I sat on the bed. "I saw you admiring the necklace. I thought you would like it," I said my voice low.

She was shaking now, tears falling slowly down her face and streaking her make-up. "You don't understand. There isn't anything wrong with the present. It's us, Julian. We are all wrong. I've tried to make it work. But we're too different. I told you from the start. I'm too young for you. You said you didn't want anything serious, but now it seems you want more. I can't give you that. I can't accept your gift. I'm sorry."

She put the necklace in my hand.

I have only cried three times in my life. The first time was when my mother died. The second time was when my wife told me she was leaving. The third time was now.

Veronica looked away, ashamed for me, or for herself. I was sure this was not the first time she had broken some poor fool's heart. Since the start of our relationship, when she flirted with me at the diner, I knew she was capable of anything, but I was weak and couldn't help myself. I bit my lip until it bled, and forced myself to stop crying.

"I understand," I said in a raspy voice. "I understand how a young girl like you would feel trapped and suffocated in a relationship with . . . with someone like me."

The bitch had the audacity to look sad. "It's not you, it's me," she said, using the standard break-up line.

"Can I ask you a favour?" I said, in such a pathetic voice she had to lean over to hear me. "Please do me the honour of going out with me tonight. One final time."

I noticed she was about to object but I pressed on. "Just for tonight. As *friends*. After that you're free to go. Tomorrow we'll go our separate ways. I can't deny how I feel about you, Veronica. It will be hard, but I'll do the right thing and let you go." I allowed my voice to break.

She sat thinking about it for a few seconds and then nodded.

"One more thing." I took the velvet case and pulled out the necklace. "Will you put it on? It was made for a princess and I can't think of anyone who would look lovelier wearing it."

She was after all a stupid, stupid little egotistical girl. She deserved all that she got threefold.

I walked behind her and she collected the strands of hair off her neck, just as I had imagined. I reached over and clasped it around her beautiful throat. It was a perfect fit. I leaned in to suck up as much of her wonderful scent as I could. The thought that her body would be denied to me after tonight, suddenly made my ribs contract against my skin with such force, that the pain almost brought me to my knees.

Except, I couldn't smell Veronica's natural odour, not with the cigar smoke and cologne and the shampoo from her freshly washed hair.

"That's too tight, Julian," she said.

"Shhh, just sit still," I said, as I triggered the secret link that latched the back of the necklace together. "There. Now don't you look stunning?"

I stood back from the mirror so she could admire herself.

She sat quietly looking at her reflection. Forgetting myself, I reached out for her hand. It was like a dead bird.

"Are you all right, my love? You look a little pale."

Her breath was deep and uneven.

"The necklace looks beautiful on you," I said. "I could see why the prince chose it for his bride."

"It's the most uncomfortable thing I have ever worn. It feels like thorns against my neck."

"Well, it looks lovely."

"I'm sorry. I should have told you how I was feeling before, Julian. I hate the way things have turned out."

"Is there someone else? Can you at least tell me that?"

"Julian . . . I thought we weren't going to talk about . . ."

"Is that a yes or a no?"

"I can't believe . . ."

"Relax, Veronica. Please sit down. I won't mention it again."

I knew it. I knew the conniving bitch had someone on the side. I suspected it weeks ago when I went to pick her up after class and she was late.

"I've had enough, Julian. I don't want to go out to dinner. I just want to take this thing off my neck."

I noticed angry blotches appearing where the necklace was rubbing against her skin.

"Fine," I said. "I just thought you would appreciate a little bit of *fun*."

"Help me take it off," she said, her hands struggling with the clasp. "It feels like it's pressing against my throat."

"Veronica, it's just a necklace."

Her breath sounding agitated.

"I can't get this damn thing off!" She fumbled futilely. "Julian, don't just stand there! Help me take it off."

"Stop struggling and let me see what I can do." I stood behind her trying to unclip the clasp the way the blond woman had demonstrated. It refused to unlock.

"Oh, my God, Julian. What did you do?"

"Nothing! Why would you think I did something?"

"It's pressing against my windpipe." She turned towards me, her eyes full of panic. "Julian, I can't breathe! It's cutting off my air supply."

"Veronica, please stand still. I can't help you if you're thrashing around."

She was gasping and coughing wildly and yanking at her neck.

"Veronica! Stop moving!" My hands were struggling but it seemed to get more tangled with my efforts to get it off her neck.

Things happened very quickly then.

Veronica clutched at her throat, her eyes bulging as if the necklace were a tourniquet. Her face was pale and her arms felt like cold marble against mine as she wrestled with the catch. She cried and pleaded for me to help, dripping spit, snot and tears. I was highly disgusted.

Then she passed out.

When she awoke later, I'd removed her dress and stretched her out on the bed, naked but still wearing the necklace.

Her hands flew to her throat. She cried out on finding it still around her neck.

"Calm down, darling."

She began to thrash around again.

"Listen, it seems to tighten the more you move, so lie still."

She screamed then. A horrible sound, like a wounded animal.

I slapped her. Harder than I wanted, but it felt good to feel her skin connect with my hand. Afterwards, she was quieter, propped on the pillows and moaning softly.

"There, there," I said, stroking her beautiful hair. "Everything is going to be all right. .I'm sorry I can't take off the necklace. You know that only true love can release you from its captivity. I guess you don't have much of a choice. You can either learn to love me again or you can keep that fucking thing around your neck for the rest of your life. It's your choice."

29 Ways to Drown

Not so long ago, before the move to London, before she tried to drown herself in Westpark Leisure Centre, Janie Summers had been a high-spirited and robust young woman who loved water. A former beach bunny and Little Miss Florida Sunshine, Janie spent most of her early life immersed in the ocean. According to her mother, she'd even been a water baby, learning to swim before she learned to walk.

Now she found she couldn't stand water in any form, couldn't swim or take showers; forced to wash herself in the sink, looking like Big Bird splashing around in his bath.

Worst of all was the sound of the rain.

In England, it rained without respite. Not just mild showers – the kind that could be banished by doing a little Gene Kelly song-and-dance number; these were big, fat vengeful raindrops – hard to ignore and even harder to dispel.

Every morning, Janie woke to the rain and every evening she went to bed with a pillow over her head, so she wouldn't hear the wind lashing outside her window. Each dawn brought with it the hope that if she sent out enough positive thoughts when she pulled back her curtains, the universe would reward her with clear blue skies. But the weather remained grim and resolute, the pale greyness stretching over the city like a cold, dead sea.

Sitting on the windowsill in her pyjamas and an old sweater, Janie watched the early commuters fight their way through the streets with their umbrellas in one hand and their cups of cardboard coffee in the other.

"I think today is a good day for a walk," said her husband, Michael, peering at her over his morning paper. "Some fresh air will do you good – dispel the doom and gloom. They aren't predicting any storms today. At most there might be a little drizzle."

"I'm not really in the mood," said Janie. "It's wet out."

"So, put on your coat. Five minutes, that's all you have to do."

"Well, that's easy for you to say. *You* don't suffer from rain-related depression." Janie's condition had become so pronounced she could hardly set foot out the door, not even to the corner store for milk and a paper.

"Dr Stevens said you should try to get out more. It's not good for you to be cooped up all the time."

"Maybe I'll go out later," said Janie. "When it stops raining." But she could tell by Michael's face that he didn't believe her.

"I'll be home late tonight. Meeting with the publishers. Do you need anything?"

"No, I have everything I need. Thanks."

"Are you sure? I can stop off somewhere before work."

"I'm *fine*. Please don't fuss, Michael."

"Listen" – he brushed back his hair with his hand – "I'm only trying to help."

"Actually, there is one thing. A question of sorts . . . When you were a little boy, did you like the *Peanuts* gang?"

He gave her a quizzical look.

"You know, the kids with the big heads? 'Good grief' and all that? The dog with the sunglasses?"

"Oh. You mean Charlie Brown?"

"Yes, but there were others: Linus, Lucy, Schroeder . . . Messed up little kids. Neurotic, but lovable."

Michael stared at her in the hallway mirror.

"Don't worry. I'm not flipping out again. I saw it on a website: 'Which Charlie Brown character are you?'"

"Oh," he sighed with relief. "In that case, I'm Snoopy. When things go wrong, I do a little dance. I don't let anything get me down for long."

Figures, she thought. Figures Michael would choose the funny and charismatic one – the *popular* character. Snoopy was too easy.

Her husband glanced at his watch. "I have to run."

"But you haven't even asked which one I am yet!"

"Later, I promise."

"Will you be home very late?"

"I'm not sure yet. Don't wait up, just in case."

"OK, then. Run along, *Snoopy*. The world awaits you." Janie stood up and attempted a Snoopy shuffle. It was meant as a joke, to make Michael smile, but one of her bedroom slippers got caught in the floorboards, making a terrible scraping sound as she dragged the other leg behind her. He froze with a horrified look on his face.

"Michael, wait," said Janie, attempting to free the slipper, but he picked up his briefcase and closed the door without a word.

After he left, she hopped back into bed, yanking the goose-down duvet over her head.

"Charlie Brown," she said to herself. "That's my character. But thanks for asking."

WHEN JANIE WAS a girl, her favourite game was one where she and her mother had tea parties under the sea. Audrey served salt water in invisible cups, while Janie patted sand together to make cakes. Then, holding their breath, both of them would submerge and sit cross-legged at the bottom of the ocean, sipping "tea" with their pinkies outstretched, until one of them giggled or ran out of breath and had to come up to the surface for air.

When Janie was ten years old, her mother died. She walked to the sea early one morning and drowned while out swimming. After that, Janie developed a phobia of water. Her father took her every weekend to the beach, hoping to ease her fears, but the little girl sat pitifully on the sand, looking out towards the ocean.

One day, months after her mother's death, Janie – without fanfare – suddenly jumped into the water, swimming out to the lighthouse and back. It was difficult to keep her out after that. In her teens, she worked as a certified lifeguard, was a member of the swim team and an avid waterskier.

It was therefore a shock to everyone, especially Michael, when six months after moving to London, she signed up for a Westpark Leisure Centre membership, put on her bathing suit, strapped on a pair of ankle weights and stepped off the deep end of the pool.

Janie let herself float down slowly until she hit the bottom. Then she crossed her legs and waited.

Dr Stevens told her that people who attempted suicide were often remarkably short-sighted, seldom having a back-up in case things didn't go to plan. How could Janie have known that the Silver Swimmers aerobics class would be occupying the pool on the same day she'd chosen to drown herself? She only cared about the smooth expanse of cool blue water followed by the strange but pleasant feeling of light-headedness.

At first, the swimmers thought Janie was just exercising

with the rest of the class, given that a lot of them also wore ankle weights. Only when she'd been submerged for longer than necessary did they notice something was wrong. The young lifeguard, only recently qualified, put his head underwater and saw Janie huddled at the bottom of the pool, her blond hair spreading out in front of her like a mermaid.

He almost dislocated her arm trying to pull her out the way the lifeguard manual said you never should. When he rose to the surface, Janie in tow, the Silver Swimmers helped lift her out, putting her down on the cold tiles, where she lay watery and lifeless.

The lifeguard put his lips to hers and clumsily administered mouth-to-mouth. After a few moments, Janie sat up in alarm, coughing and sputtering water. The lifeguard was so relieved he looked as if he were going to cry.

"Are you all right?" he kept asking.

Janie, her eyes and throat stinging from the chlorine, wanted to answer, but her tongue felt shrivelled and dry. She could taste salt water on her lips, although she knew that was impossible.

"Hush, don't try to speak," the instructor of the water-aerobics class said. "Your lungs are probably smarting." She gently patted her hand.

As they waited for the ambulance to arrive, Janie felt time slow down. Someone removed her ankle weights and placed a towel around her legs. Someone else placed a bottle of water beside her. She could see the lifeguard's trembling hands, the kindly face of the instructor, the accusatory eyes of some of the elderly swimmers, even her own blue toes peeking out from the towel.

"Sorry," Janie whispered to the teenage lifeguard and to the aerobics class as the paramedics put her on a gurney. "I'm so very, very sorry."

Later, at the hospital, she was put on an IV so she wouldn't dehydrate, and wrapped in warm blankets. But she wouldn't stop shivering. Michael rushed in, saw his waterlogged wife and couldn't speak. He just looked at her, touching her head and hands lightly, as if he couldn't believe she was alive.

WHEN SHE WAS released from the hospital, Janie slept for days at a time. Between states of sleep and unconsciousness, she wasn't sure what was real and what was a dream. She was so exhausted, she didn't have the energy to pull herself to the surface to find out; she just let herself fall deeper and deeper.

Janie had fallen asleep under the duvet. She was having one of her strange recurring dreams again. She was swimming in the ocean, her eyes open underwater and she could see beautiful exotic fish all around. She swam deeper, her hair floating back and forth in front of her like seaweed. The next thing she knew, her father was in the water, stripped to his underclothes. He pulled Janie out and then they were by the side of the Westpark pool.

"Kid," her father said, "you messed up. You messed up real bad. But it isn't the end of the world. You are tougher than you give yourself credit for – and smarter. Don't you know there are only twenty-nine ways to drown? Number twenty-three, throwing yourself into a pool full of people, with a lifeguard and a fully booked water-aerobics class, is just plain dumb."

Her father had an old army book about water survival, called *29 Ways to Drown*. As a kid, Janie was fascinated by the stick-figure illustrations explaining how to avoid water-related injuries: "1. Don't swim when tired. 2. Don't stand on the edge of a boat when drinking. 3. Don't fall asleep in the bath." The book even gave advice in case you accidentally fell into a lake ("4. Don't get hypothermia.") and explained how bracing water helped protect the body against drowning.

"Next time," said her dream father, "try an isolated lake and remember to fill your pockets with stones."

Janie sat up with a start, surprised to find that only a few hours had elapsed since Michael had left for work.

She got up, put on her robe and made herself some toast, eating it standing by the window. Her days were like this now, one running seamlessly into the other. Janie wondered what Michael would say if she told him she wanted to leave London and move back home. Would he accompany her as he'd promised or would he realise once and for all that they weren't meant to be?

THEY HAD MET at a Key West seminar where Michael was promoting his book, *Responsible 21st-Century Travel and You*. He stepped up to the podium to deliver his talk in front of three hundred attendees, most of them from the travel industry, with the opening line, "I just flew in from London and boy, are my arms tired."

Janie felt a jolt run from the roots of her hair, past her kneecaps and down to her toes. How could she be attracted to a man whose philosophy was that people shouldn't wander around the world senselessly globetrotting?

As a writer for a popular woman's magazine, Janie was a vivacious, independent traveller, having exotic adventures and living out of a travel bag. She brushed her teeth in airports and carried extra underwear in her purse. Back then, she wasn't afraid of anything.

During the Q&A portion of his talk, Janie raised her hand and asked Michael a question about the ozone layer. It was a lame attempt to get him to notice her, but he smiled and replied in a way that didn't make her feel stupid.

Later, when the audience congregated in the main hall to mingle and have drinks, Janie sought Michael out and positioned herself in an alcove behind a potted plant so she could watch him. With his dark hair and his lightly tanned skin contrasting against his denim shirt, she had to admit he was good-looking. He had possibly the best lips she had ever seen on a man: well shaped and expressive, the mouth of a sensual kisser. She realised too late that Michael was watching her.

Stay calm, Janie, stay calm, she said to herself. He probably hasn't noticed you're spying on him.

"Hello there," said Michael, standing over the plant. "I didn't recognise you with the foliage. Is that a new look?"

"I hope you don't think I'm some weirdo stalker." She laughed nervously.

"Are you sure?" he asked with mock disappointment. "I know a few colleagues who would be very excited to hear I had groupies – or at least a fan. Makes a change from the usual hate mail."

Janie was at a loss for words. Her face flushed and the palms of her hands grew sweaty like an adolescent in the throes of a puppy crush. "I'm sure you don't get that much hate mail."

"Yes. Yes, I'm afraid I do. Especially from people in the travel industry. We usually place last in the popularity stakes. Right after politicians, lawyers and hippies."

"I thought you *were* a hippy," she said.

"We prefer the term 'eco-warrior', thank you very much. It's ever so rakish and adventurous-sounding, don't you think?"

"Eco-warrior sounds like an Earth-friendly cologne."

"Actually, to be honest, I'm not even that. I teach environmental science. I leave the hard-core things to the activists," he said, laughing. His laughter was deep and warm; it made Janie's ribcage contract.

"What do you do . . . *Janie*?" he asked, leaning in to read her nametag.

"I'm a travel writer. A globetrotter. The enemy of your people, you might say. But, you know, at home I try to recycle. I know it sounds insignificant, but I really do."

"May I ask you a personal question, Janie?"

"I don't know why I love travelling," she blurted out. "I guess it's in my blood. It's my livelihood, my reason for being and yes, I do know how bad it is for the environment."

"That wasn't my question."

"Oh. Sorry. My mistake. Shall we try again?"

"Do I make you uncomfortable?"

"Uhm. No. Not really. Well, yes. Maybe a *little*."

"Look, I'm not going to apologise for what I do. But I'm not a monk or a priest. There is no one right way to live your life." He fixed his hazel eyes on her until she was forced to look away. "Those of us who fly have to make up for it in other ways. That's why I wrote the book. It's about taking responsibility and not letting guilt ground you – excuse the pun."

"Well, I'm afraid that's not an option for me. I suffer from incurable wanderlust. Everywhere sounds better than home."

"So where do you live?"

"Here in Key West, for now. But I hate to come home to an empty house, so I'm always moving."

"What you need is a loving pet or a good houseplant. I have one in my office that is a confidant and a friend. He is a fern and goes by the name of Oscar P. Goodwin."

"I can't have a plant. I'm not home long enough. I don't even want to imagine the consequences. God forbid I should get a pet."

"You're right. Better not. It could get ugly."

"So why three names for a common houseplant?"

"Common? Oh, I'm glad Oscar P. is not around to hear that."

She laughed. "I hope I'm not monopolising you."

"No, not at all. I'm quite enjoying our conversation."

"So, have you managed to see much of Key West yet?"

"I'm afraid I've been too busy."

"How about the beach? It's beautiful at night."

"Sounds great."

"Well, what are we waiting for?" Janie said.

They left the conference and walked towards the beach hand in hand.

"Sometimes I come here late at night and walk beside the water. The salty air is good for clearing your head." Janie looked up at the sky. "Have you ever been skinny-dipping?"

"Is that like body painting?" he said smiling.

"Sort of. Would you like to try it?" She pulled off her top and threw it on the sand. "Well come on, don't just stand there." She ran to the sea, leaving a trail of discarded clothing. Right before Janie got in the water, she stood for a few seconds under the moonlight, letting the evening air hit her naked skin. Then, gracefully, she dived into a white-crested wave, emerging from the water sleek as a seal.

"It's the perfect temperature," she cried out, floating on her back and looking at the stars.

"Janie, ahem . . . Are there any sharks in these parts?" Michael said from the shore.

"This time of year it's unlikely. Besides, they aren't as bad as people make them out to be. They're more frightened of us than we are of them. They prefer tuna to human flesh, anyway."

"Right. That's reassuring."

"Michael, you do know that skinny-dipping means you have to take your clothes off, right?"

"Yes, of course. I know. I'm dying to join you. I really want to. But I can't. See, the thing is, I don't know how to swim."

"What?"

"I don't know how to swim. Don't look at me like that. It

isn't like I confessed to eating dolphins or anything."

She disappeared under the water.

"Janie. Janie, where are you?"

She popped up again. "Sorry, just making sure there aren't any sharks."

"Don't say that. I was traumatised when I saw *Jaws* as a kid. I refused to go into the pool. 'Dear Teacher. Please excuse Michael from lessons. He has complete paralytic aquaphobia.' I don't, mind you. I just don't like the ocean. Or swimming," he added as an afterthought.

"You poor thing. And yet here you are. Wait, I'll make my way to you."

She appeared on the sand, her skin glistening in the moonlight. Michael fumbled with his shoes and socks, trying not to gawp.

"Here, take my hand," she said, leading him slowly into the water.

"Wait," he said, rolling up his trouser legs. "OK, ready. I'm better now than I used to be, you know. I couldn't even get into the water when I was a kid. Careful, up to my knees is the limit. After that it gets ugly: sweats, palpitations. I've even been known to pass out."

"Isn't this romantic?"

"Fantastic. Perfect. The water, the temperature, the stars . . . It is all wonderful. But please, can we go back now?"

"Of course," Janie said.

Back on shore, Michael offered her his denim shirt and turned away politely so Janie could dry herself. His shirt smelled like orange blossoms and salty sea air.

"You were brave to go into the water."

"I took a chance," he said, putting on his shoes. He smiled at her and took her hand as they walked up the pathway.

"I've had such a great time. I don't want to go home."

At the door to her apartment, he put his arms around her and kissed her on both cheeks. He was right about one thing, Janie thought, as she fumbled with her keys and unlocked the door. Everything about that night was perfect. At that moment in his arms, she was exactly where she wanted to be.

WHEN THEY STARTED dating and commuting across the ocean, Janie felt her life was as romantic and unbelievably cosmopolitan and grown-up as one of her travel articles. They met in Paris, London and Berlin, on trains, buses, ferries and once or twice on a bicycle. She was wonderfully, hopelessly in love. But every time she returned to the US, or worse, when Michael left her, she felt the same familiar lump of uncertainty and loneliness in her stomach.

Things changed when he started working on a new book focusing on climate change in North America. Janie was ecstatic. It meant they could spend time together while he did his research. But within weeks he was homesick, missing his family, friends, the smell of the countryside, even the rain. Michael had been born, gone to school and lived in the same place his entire life; of course he was going to miss it. Pretty soon, though, it wasn't just his friends and family he longed for. He began to grow sentimental for other things: Sunday roasts, English lager, cricket and other cultural aspects of British life taken off the shelf of his memories like prized trophies to be polished and admired.

This was hard for Janie to comprehend, although she knew that seemingly trivial connections sometimes pointed to bigger things that one could not articulate. And it wasn't enough that Janie, trying to surprise him, had taken him to the Lion's Head, an English pub in Fort Meyers. They ordered fish and chips and mushy peas, and while Michael agreed it was delicious, he became even more wistful for the *authentic* stuff – authentic, in his case, meaning three thousand miles across the ocean.

One day she came home and found him clutching a small object to his chest. She grew alarmed when she saw the shredded brown paper on the table, evidence of a package from home. She sat gently next to him and took his hand in hers. Michael showed her what he was cradling in his hand like a momma-less baby bird.

"Look," he said, showing her a broken Oxo cube. "They came like that. All of them! Pulverised, as if they had kicked it all the way from the warehouse. *Savages*."

Janie tried to stop herself from laughing, but the giggles escaped through her nose like champagne bubbles. "And here I thought something awful happened!" she said putting her arms around him.

"It did," he said. "Don't laugh. It isn't funny. When I was little, my mum used to make mashed potatoes and gravy whenever I didn't feel well. I told her Oxo cubes were difficult to get here so she sent them special delivery. She even sent her special gravy recipe. I was going to cook some for you tonight."

"We'll eat something else. We'll order in. You know, I'm not really crazy about gravy. In fact, to be honest, I *hate* it."

"Hate gravy? How could you hate gravy?"

"It's brown and gooey and it drowns the flavour of food."

"That's terrible, Janie. A civilised person shouldn't have to go without gravy. Gravy is the mainstay that binds together English cuisine. Having dinner without gravy is as un-English as Christmas without crackers."

"Yeah, about that . . . I don't get that whole Christmas-cracker thing either."

"I can't believe you are saying that." His voice rose. "You are supposed to be an enlightened person, an open-minded woman who has been everywhere and tried everything."

"Yes, but that doesn't mean I have to like what you like."

"Well, maybe I need to reassess why I like *you*."

"You don't mean that, Michael."

"Gravy is part of my upbringing. I mean, if you can't understand that, how can you ever understand me?" He crossed his arms and refused to look at her.

She thought he was joking at first. Here they were having the first big fight of their relationship and it was about something as silly as gravy. But the stubborn look on his face said otherwise. For a minute, doubt clouded Janie's mind. What had at first seemed like the perfect relationship was all of a sudden full of differences so obvious and wide, they were like giant craters.

In the morning he was contrite. "I was silly, Janie. I'm sorry."

He put his arms around her and kissed the top of her head and everything was fine again. But a small nagging hole, like a cigarette butt, had burned into the fabric of her happiness.

"MOVE TO ENGLAND with me," Michael said after they'd been together for eight months. "The book is almost finished and I have to go back soon. I don't want to be away from you." They lay reading the paper, their legs entwined on the couch. "What do you say, Janie?"

"I don't know, Michael. I like London, but it is crowded and chaotic. I would really prefer somewhere near the sea."

He grimaced. "I know, but it's home."

"I can't imagine living in a place where it rains all the time. I'd get bored or go crazy. I'd get claustrophobic."

"Bored? It doesn't rain *all* the time, Janie."

"I thought you liked Florida."

"I do, but I feel I've done my time," he said, as if Key

West were a prison, instead of the paradise he'd once told her it was.

They disentangled their legs and moved to separate sides of the couch.

They'd had this conversation before. They'd even had a version where Michael asked Janie to marry him. But she didn't want to move. Since meeting him, she'd made friends and settled down in Key West. She had a life there, a favourite coffee place; she even had plants.

"I love you, Janie. I don't want to be without you. Please, can you at least try it for a few months? If you don't like it, we'll come back here or go wherever you want. I just want to be with you."

In the end she agreed to both the marriage and the move. She sorted out the necessary paperwork, sold her bike and camping equipment and donated her books to a charity shop. Looking around her empty apartment she had a sinking feeling in her heart. But she loved Michael; how could she not at least try to be happy in London?

As their plane flew across the Atlantic, Janie squeezed Michael's hand and tried not to cry.

IN MAY, IT finally stopped raining. Janie agreed to leave their flat on a beautiful Saturday morning, Michael having persuaded her to take a walk around the park. He even made some sandwiches in case they felt like a picnic.

"Wait," she said, as they were at the door. She rushed back into the house and Michael sighed, but she came out again with a plastic bag full of bread crusts for the ducks. As the bright light hit her, she shielded her eyes, feeling as if she hadn't been outside in years.

The park was bustling with children, their parents, dogs, runners and a herd of skateboarders with floppy hair.

"Baby steps, Janie," Michael kept saying. "Just take baby steps. Soon you will be back to your normal self, zipping around the park on your bike and rollerblading."

But after only a few minutes outside, she felt exhausted. "I want to go home now."

"Already? But we just came out."

"Please. I've had enough."

"OK. But let's feed the ducks first," he said as if talking to a small child. "You wanted to see the ducks, right?"

She nodded. He held her hand and they slowly made their way around to the pond.

"Don't get too close, Janie."

"Michael, I'm not an infant."

"I know. It's just . . ."

"If I were stupid enough to fall in, I *can* swim, you know."

He stared at her as if she was being unreasonable.

"I am an adult. I haven't been acting like one lately, but I assure you, I can be quite grown-up when I want to be."

"I'm just trying to help," he said in a hurt voice.

"Well, don't," she snapped. "I can manage on my own."

She had apologised to Michael at least a hundred times, wanting things to go back to the way they were in the early days of their relationship. She admitted what she had done was senseless and stupid; she had reassured, explained, been counselled and all the doctors agreed she was getting better. No one knew exactly the cause of her latent depression, least of all Janie.

"You shouldn't blame yourself," the doctor told Janie at her last appointment. "The important thing is that you are alive and fighting to stay healthy. That's all anyone can hope for. Just take one day at a time . . ."

She had had enough. She wanted her life back. She was damned if she was going to live this way, coddled, protected, treated as if she were a delicate invalid at death's door.

"I want to walk around the perimeter – *by myself*, Michael. This is just as much about letting me be independent and self-sufficient as it is about getting me out of the house."

"Fine," he said. "But I'll be close by if you need me."

She started walking in the other direction, slowly making her way around the path. She didn't turn, but she knew if she did, she would find Michael trailing behind her.

Janie closed her eyes, letting the warmth of the sun brush her pale shoulders. The day was gorgeous, warm and sunny. She didn't remember many glorious days in London and this one was like a special treat. Florida floated vague and undefined in her memories, almost every day a perfect, assembly-line blue. So why did she feel so depressed when she thought of going back home?

She pulled out the plastic bag holding the breadcrumbs. Having walked to the edge of the pond she threw the crusts into the air like confetti. One duck refused to join the others in the quest for food. Janie wondered if he was hurt. She inched closer to investigate.

"Are you tangled up, bird?"

There was a sudden rush of angry fluttering and then he was off – not hurt after all.

Janie realised with a start that she was standing in the pond. Panicked, she tried to scramble on to the embankment, lost her footing, and landed – bottom first – in the water with a giant splash. There was another mad rush of feathers and squawking, as the rest of the ducks moved away from the intruder.

Janie sat in water heavy with moss, scum, bird poo and God knew what else, her trousers and shoes completely ruined.

She looked up to see a quick dark movement behind an oak tree.

Michael.

Without seeing him, she could imagine his mortified face. For a moment, Janie didn't know whether to burst into tears or start laughing. It hit her with a wave of sadness that he probably thought she really was crazy. He said he forgave her and still loved her, but she knew the truth. He would always lurk, suspicious and wary, wondering if he should hide the bath plugs in case she wanted to drown herself in the tub. And then what? The knives in the kitchen drawers? Forbidding her to do dishes in the sink? Where would distrust and suspicion end? She giggled as she imagined eating forever off disposable plates with plastic utensils.

The few clouds in the sky dispersed, revealing a perfect blue day. The afternoon sun shone brilliantly, its rays warming her back and shoulders, as Janie threw back her head and laughed, splashing like a duck in the dirty pond water, deciding whether she should sink or swim.